Through the ever-changing
and ever changeable Time
That was once Mine.

LAILA AND THE SANDS OF TIME

SHIRIN SHAMSI

Edited by
AUSTIN RUH

Summary: Thirteen-year-old Laila, still grieving over her father's death, goes
on their planned pilgrimage with her aunt and uncle. When she is
transported back in time to 7th century Arabia, she faces the dangers of the
desert, takes on a disguise, and saves a baby's life. But will she ever return to
her own time?

Clear Fork Publishing

P.O. Box 870

102 S. Swenson

Stamford, Texas 79553

(325)773-5550

www.clearforkpublishing.com

Printed and Bound in the United States of America.

ISBN - 978-1-946101-77-8

For Nadia, Sabeen, Shaheed,
- May faith and hope be your constant companions in Life's journey.

PROLOGUE

LAILA RACED FRANTICALLY toward the cry. A baby's cry that pierced the still silence of a moonless night. A wind picked up, rippling through the sand. Its soft whistle steadily increased in force, turning into a fierce and angry howl. It was as if all the forces in the universe cried out against a great injustice. Laila forged forward, determined. The wind whipped and lashed against her. She did not falter, though she felt the force of a sea of swirling sand. She braced herself, grabbing her jacket tighter as she pulled it over her head. A taste of bitter, gritty sand burned her throat. Her eyes stung from its sharpness. She waded on, squinting through the desert darkness. The cry grew closer and louder with each step forward. *Almost there!* she whispered. And the wailing wind carried her voice across the dunes and far into the night. Wrapped in a shroud, a small bundle lay on the sand. It moved. A scream ripped through the howling storm.

CHAPTER 1
PACKING

Laila pulled the closet open and dragged out her suitcase. In just a few hours she would be leaving with her aunt and uncle. She stood gazing at the sunlight-dappled patterns, as they danced across her bedroom wall, and wondered if going on pilgrimage was even a good idea.

She unzipped the suitcase and sighed. Would going all the way on Pilgrimage, *Umrah,* fix everything that was wrong in her life? She was going for Baba, her father. It was what they had planned together, before her whole world turned upside down.

Laila glanced at the clock on the wall. It was only 6:00 a.m. She watched the seconds tick by. Her eyes clouded over as she remembered. Would that she could turn back time. Back two years – before Baba remarried, before he got sick, before everything changed. But she was not a time-traveler like Doctor Who, nor did she have a TARDIS.

She stared out her bedroom window. Everything looked the same. Out front, the maple tree stood tall with its bare branches spread wide. Spring was late again in Chicago. A tire swing moved in the soft early-morning breeze, suspended by thick ropes. She turned away from the window, blinking back tears. A prayer mat sat folded in the corner, collecting dust, unused since Baba died. She had missed *Fajr*—the morning prayer—again. The thought tugged at her heart, for she didn't want to let Baba down.

Her gaze came to rest upon a photograph on the night-stand by her bed. A framed picture of Baba with Laila on her thirteenth birthday, taken before he was diagnosed with lung cancer. Baba's arm rested on her shoulder, his face lit up with joy. He looked so alive, yet the cancer had eaten away at him, and within four months he would be gone. Laila's smile was wide in the photograph, her eyes sparkling.

She decided she could never feel happy again, as she was in that photograph. Picking up the photograph, she wrapped it tenderly in the soft folds of her mother's *hijab,* then slid it into her backpack. She would take this memento of her mother to wear on Pilgrimage.

Laila pulled herself up and rummaged in her closet, grabbing a shirt and jeans to wear to school. It was the last day before spring break.

Tiptoeing slowly down the stairs, Laila hoped no one had woken up yet. She avoided her stepmom when she could. Raisa was already there in the kitchen when Laila walked in. She greeted Laila with a smile. She stood tall and slim, a shawl draped around her shoulders.

"*Salaam Alaikum,* Laila," she said. "You're up early." Laila's stepmom stood by the stove warming up some milk for baby Naila.

"I need to pack before school," said Laila, as a frown furrowed her forehead. She turned away, impatient, as she grabbed a glass and filled it with water. She gulped it down quickly, and left the kitchen before Raisa could ask anything more. Running back upstairs, Laila stood, staring at her suit-case, then shrugged and decided she would pack later. She grabbed her backpack and trudged downstairs. Slipping on her shoes and jacket, she breathed a sigh, muttered a good-bye, and left the house. At least on pilgrimage she would be away from them. She had to get away. It was hard enough without Baba, but worse having the daily reminder of her stepmom and Naila.

CHAPTER 2
SCHOOL

Two-year-old Laila searched from room to room.

"Mama," she said, as she looked around in confusion. Baba scooped her up in his arms. "Hush my Beti, I'm here with you," Baba whispered softly. He rocked her gently as he sang a lullaby. Moments later, Laila slept peacefully. Her soft, chubby hand clasped her mother's scarf, resting it close against her cheek, for it had been only weeks since her mother left the world. Her fragrance and memories still resided in their home and painfully in their hearts.

LAILA STARED AT THE DOODLES SHE HAD IDLY DRAWN across her science notebook.

"Students, I have a great surprise for you all," Mrs. Mullings announced. She rubbed her hands together, looking far more excited than the students appeared. "We will be taking part in a DNA experiment. Just think of how a strand of hair, or a drop of saliva, holds the key to your history. Science is the most thrilling mystery!" Mrs. Mullings' enthusiasm was contagious. Soon the whole class was abuzz with chatter as she patiently answered each of their questions.

"We will be going to the Field Museum's DNA Discovery Center on the 17th of next month. Where we get to take part in a new scientific breakthrough in DNA research and go on a guided tour of the lab to witness real scientists at work. It's all so very exciting. And finally—" she added, looking at the clock. "Oh dear, time is running out, but I can't leave you all in suspense for the entire spring break. We will *all* get to have our DNA tests done!" The hum of excitement in the classroom rose, as the bell rang to announce the end of the school day. There was a sudden scraping of chairs and a scurry to hurry out of class.

"Enjoy your break everyone. Stay safe. See you next month," said Mrs. Mullings. "And don't forget to read chapter ten on DNA, pages 213 to 265," she added.

Laila slammed her book shut and pushed out her chair. She swung her backpack over her shoulder and followed Beth out the door. Kids thronged the hallway as more spilled out from other classrooms. Lockers opened and slammed shut as everyone emptied their contents in haste to leave for the start of their break. Laila caught up with Beth at the staircase.

"Hey Laila, you're leaving tonight, aren't you?" Beth said as they walked down the stairs together.

"Yeah, and I haven't even packed yet," Laila replied as two boys hurriedly zipped passed them.

"I can help. Is it okay if I come over?" Beth asked as she looked at Laila.

"Thanks, that'd be great," Laila said with a sigh.

"You okay, Laila?" Beth asked. There was concern in her voice. Laila had not been herself of late.

"I'm just wondering if going on a pilgrimage to Mecca is a good idea after all. My dad wanted to take me. Now I'm going with my aunt and uncle. It won't be the same..." Laila didn't finish her sentence. It was too painful to remember that just over a year ago, she would have gone with Baba.

"Maybe it'll help, just going there—it might be just what you need," Beth said. "You said yourself that you need to get away." Beth was the one constant in her life, which had turned upside down in the last four months.

"Excuse me, Laila," Miss Levin's voice broke into their conversation. Laila turned to find herself face to face with her Social Studies teacher. She stifled a groan, remembering why Miss Levin was there.

"I hope you have not forgotten your report Laila. It's important for you to do the research." Miss Levin never smiled. "Everyone has handed them in, except you." Her face was stern as she waited for Laila to reply.

"Miss Levin, I'll have it by next week. I mean after spring break," Laila said.

"I will give you the extra week then," said Miss Levin, and she walked away.

"Why has she got it in for me?" asked Laila, shaking her head in frustration.

"It's not you. She's like that with everyone," Beth said. "You better get working on the report. What topic have you chosen?"

"I haven't really thought about it," Laila said as she pushed through the door at the school's exit.

"Maybe you'll find some ideas on pilgrimage," Beth said as they made their way out of the school.

The two friends walked down the sidewalk that led to Main Street. They crossed the road together, and soon turned the corner onto Dunkeld Road.

"Thanks, Beth. You rock," Laila said gratefully, as she pulled out her key and turned it in the front door of 4221, the place that had been home for the last thirteen years.

Pungent flavors of cinnamon and cloves wafted through

the air. *Murgh Pullao,* rice with chicken, both her and Baba's favorite dish. Baba had made it every weekend for as long as Laila could remember. That is, until he remarried. Both girls slipped off their shoes. Laila dropped her bag to the ground as her stepmom appeared from the kitchen.

"*Salaam Alaikum,* Laila. Hello, Beth," Raisa said with a warm smile. "I've made dinner early, so we can eat right away if you like."

"Hi, Mrs. Saleem. Thanks, it smells delicious," said Beth.

"Um, we're in a hurry," Laila said abruptly. "Beth's helping me pack, and we're not that hungry." Laila's voice was cold as she ignored the gentle whisperings of her conscience. She held tightly onto the anger and resentment toward her stepmom. Avoiding her stepmom's sad face, Laila turned, picked up her bag, then ran upstairs. Beth sighed wistfully as she breathed in the succulent smells emanating from the kitchen. Reluctantly, she followed Laila upstairs to her bedroom.

"I could eat now. I'm starving," said Beth gloomily.

"If you don't mind, we need to pack first," Laila said, pulling open the suitcase that sat in the middle of the rug on the floor.

"Sure," said Beth. "I'm here to help, but the food smells so good." She looked at Laila, who stood before her open closet and surveyed its contents. "What's the temperature like?"

Laila pulled out her phone and Googled the weather. "Saudi Arabia's average temperature for this time of year can go up to 140 degrees Fahrenheit," she said, reading the weather report from her phone. She grabbed a few T-shirts and two pairs of faded blue jeans, throwing them into the suitcase. Next, she added a bag of toiletries and an inhaler, hoping her asthma would be under control while there. Once, she went to Karachi with Baba, his place of birth in Pakistan. She was eight at the time and had to be hospitalized due to an asthma attack. She could not afford to have that happen again.

"Are you packing jeans and T-shirts to wear in Mecca? Even I know that's not going to fly in one of the holiest cities in the world!" Beth said. Laila grinned.

"Aunt Balqees is bringing me some head scarves and maxi-length *abayas,*" Laila said, chuckling. "I'll wear T-shirts and jeans under the *abaya.*"

"What about the pilgrimage, what do you call it?" Beth asked, as she sat down on the rug and pulled out a T-shirt, proceeding to fold it and roll it up.

"*Umrah* is the shorter pilgrimage," said Laila.

"Yeah, so what will you wear for the *Umrah?*" Beth asked as she folded the T-shirts and then went on to fold Laila's jeans.

"I'll wear the same long *abaya* and *hijab* over a T-shirt and jeans," said Laila. "Maybe I should take some cotton pants. They'll be cooler than denim. And thanks for folding my stuff and helping."

"Laila, Beth..." Laila's stepmom called from downstairs. "Are you two coming down? They'll be here soon." Laila muttered a reply and closed her suitcase roughly.

"I guess you should eat before you go on a 12-hour flight?" Beth said.

"I couldn't eat a thing," said Laila with a groan, as she pressed her hand to her stomach. She was nervous and afraid. Her hopes were set on this trip—hopes of finding the faith her Baba had. Yet she feared going without him. "I'll throw up for sure."

Beth checked the contents of Laila's suitcase. "We have jeans and T-shirts nicely folded," said Beth. "Anything else?"

"All done," said Laila.

Both Laila and Beth joined Raisa in the kitchen. Ten-month-old Naila was seated in her high-chair, waving her spoon in the air as her mom spooned rice and chicken into a plastic bowl. She looked up with a smile at both Laila and Beth.

"I made chicken-rice," Raisa said, "your favorite. As a going away treat."

"Thanks, I'm not hungry," Laila mumbled, as knots twisted in her stomach. How could she enjoy the food she had shared with Baba? "It won't taste as good as Baba's, and besides it's called *Murgh Pullao*," Laila muttered, though only Beth heard.

As the four of them sat together for their evening meal, Laila was quiet, and barely took a bite. Beth tried her best to make conversation.

"Thanks for the dinner, it was so good," Beth said, as she rose to leave.

"You're welcome anytime," said Raisa warmly. She grabbed the baby from the high-chair, Naila's chubby face was covered with sticky rice. Laila walked Beth to the front door.

Beth slipped on her shoes and whispered, "Why do you ignore your sister? And you're downright rude to your stepmom." Laila shook her head.

"I don't know," she said as her voice shook. She looked down at her hands, clasping and unclasping them nervously. "I just can't forget that they took away my time with my dad." Laila's tears fell freely. She could not shake the grief that gnawed at her and at times overwhelmed her. Beth hugged her.

"Look, my mom says it takes time. Grieving. And sometimes it's easier to blame someone else because you don't know what to do with the pain," said Beth. "But don't change who you are, Laila. Don't change the person I know, who cried when Davey killed a spider." Laila's black eyes glistened with tears. She smiled as she remembered the incident. She was known as spider-girl after her meltdown over the death of a spider.

"See you next week!" Beth said. The two friends fist-bumped each other. A car drew up as Laila watched Beth walk down the street. Laila wiped her tears with the back of her arm. *They're here!* She ran upstairs to her bedroom, grabbed her suitcase, pulled it by the handle and dragged it out the door. She turned and looked around the room one more time, then wheeled her suitcase down the stairs, to her waiting aunt and uncle.

Aunt Balqees smiled and hugged Laila, holding her for a few moments longer than necessary as she took in Laila's wan face.

"You've lost weight," she said. "Haven't you been eating Laila?" Uncle Farid walked in with a smile.

"*Salaam, Beti*, are you ready for an adventure?" He said, though his casual manner belied the tenderness with which he searched Laila's face. He wrapped her in a warm hug and kissed her forehead. "We've only got a few minutes, so if you want to say your goodbyes now, go ahead."

"*Assalaam-Alaikum,* Raisa *Bhabi*," Uncle Farid said, his voice husky with emotion, as he reached forward and grabbed Naila from Raisa's arms. Naila chirped with glee as he bounced her on his shoulders.

"*Walaikum-Assalaam*," Raisa replied. A wave of sadness washed over Uncle Farid's face. At 33, Raisa was too young to be a widow, his brother's widow. The air was heavy with an uncomfortable presence of an unspoken loss. Baba was there, at the forefront of everyone's mind, yet no one mentioned him. It was too soon, and still too painful for the daughter, the wife, and the younger brother.

Naila giggled as Uncle Farid swung her up and down.

"Here you go, give your big sister a kiss," he said, handing her to Laila. Laila's arms stiffened as she felt Naila's soft chubbiness against her. "La-La," cooed Naila, demanding attention as she pressed her lips to Laila's face. The soggy wetness of the baby's kiss almost melted Laila's heart, if she would let it. But she had built a fortress of resentment to fill the void left in her life, not knowing how else to cope.

Uncle Farid and Aunt Balqees bade their farewell greetings and wheeled Laila's suitcase to the car. Raisa held Naila on her hip as they both watched Laila slip on her shoes, ready to leave.

"We'll miss you Laila," said Raisa. "If Naila were a little older, we'd come with you." She put her arms around Laila, who stood stiffly with her arms firmly by her side. Laila breathed a sigh of relief, thankful they were not able to go with her. "*Fi-Amman-Allah,* God protect you," were her stepmom's last words to her as she walked out the door to the waiting car. The sorrow in her heart weighed heavy upon her. It wove itself into her veins and stared from the depth of her deep black eyes. Laila was overwhelmed by a grief not easily lifted. She sat in the car and did not turn around to see Naila waving at her from her mother's arms.

CHAPTER 3
MECCA

Eleven-year-old Laila pushed a cart in the grocery store with Baba. She chose a box of cereal and added it to the pile of groceries in the shopping cart.

"What was it like Baba, when you and Mama went on your honeymoon?" asked Laila.

"Well—we didn't— we decided to go on pilgrimage to Mecca for a new start to our married life together." Baba replied. He looked in the distance. A smile hovered on his mouth as he remembered fondly, with feelings of sadness and gladness intermingled.

"Can we go? Just you and I?" asked Laila.

"God willing, before the year is out, I will take you," Baba said. "It's an experience you will not forget. When you stand before your Creator, then everything falls into place. You feel like a small atom in the vast universe. You feel your place in all creation, for everything is connected, and you find peace."

The flight was long and tedious. Laila had the window seat, so for a while she stared at clouds. She watched a movie, then slept intermittently for the duration of the flight. About forty minutes before landing, the flight attendant announced:

"For those passengers planning on pilgrimage, we will soon be entering the *Miqat* area, so be advised to make preparations."

Uncle Farid awoke upon hearing the announcement. He unbuckled his belt and stood up.

"What did the attendant mean?" Laila asked.

"This is where we change into *Ihram*," Uncle Farid said. "*Miqat* is the point where you change into the simple pilgrim's dress." He grabbed his bag from the overhead bin and walked down the aisle to the restrooms.

Moments later when Uncle Farid returned, Laila had to look twice before realizing her normally suited uncle was wearing two white pieces of toweling fabric wrapped around him. Aunt Balqees left her seat, taking her bag with her. She changed out of her shirt and jeans into a long, buttoned-down, maxi-length coat. Instead of her blue-patterned *hijab,* she now wore a plain, cream-colored headscarf.

"I've brought an *abaya* just like this for you, Laila," Aunt Balqees said. She opened her duffle bag and rummaged through it pulling out a bundle of clothes. She handed the neatly folded clothes to Laila, "Here you go. It's a roomy restroom, so you can change quite easily."

Laila took the clothes and walked to the restroom, where she waited in line. It seemed like everyone needed to use the restroom. She breathed a sigh of relief when her turn came. Clearly this was designed for pilgrims. There was a shower stall and plenty of room to wash and dress. Laila held up the clothes her aunt had brought for her. It was very plain—simply a long, buttoned-down tunic. She washed and changed into the pale-cream *abaya*. Instead of the *hijab* her aunt gave her, Laila took out her mother's soft cotton scarf and donned it on her head, adding two pins to secure

it. As she adjusted her scarf, she stared at her reflection.
Her large, black eyes looked way too big for her face. Aunt
Balqees was right, she had lost weight. It felt strange to be
in a *hijab* and *abaya*. Laila felt like she was looking at
someone else.

"You look very elegant," said Aunt Balqees.

"And very grown up," added Uncle Farid with a smile.

The pilot announced they were about to land. He first
spoke in Arabic, then English.

"I envy you Laila," said Aunt Balqees. "You speak Arabic
so fluently, we will have to rely on you to be our guide here."

"Yes, *Maasha'Allah*, it is such a great gift to know the
language," Uncle Farid said, as Laila took her seat by the
window. She wondered how it would be, pilgrimage without
Baba. She sighed and leaned back in her seat, as the plane
began its descent.

From the airport, Laila, with her aunt and uncle, took a
taxi to the hotel. Laila gazed at the views as the taxi whizzed
along the highway. They passed skyscrapered skylines interspersed with barren desert, dotted by palm trees.

"It's just over an hour from Jeddah to Mecca," Uncle Farid
said. Laila dozed off, leaning against the soft cushioned back-
seat of the car. The air-conditioning felt soothing, and its
sound lulled her to sleep.

They arrived at the hotel, and were soon checked in.

"It's not as grand as the hotels near the Grand Mosque,"
said Uncle Farid, "but we can handle the walk from here to
the Grand Mosque."

"There's no way we can afford the luxury hotels near the
Kaaba," Aunt Balqees said. It was all too much luxury for her
liking.

As her aunt and uncle waited for the elevator, Laila took
the stairs two at a time. The elevator was way too slow. Stum-
bling over the hem of her *abaya,* she pulled it up with both

hands and sprinted up the last stretch of the hotel's marble staircase.

"This is so bulky," she muttered. "How does anyone walk in it, let alone run?" Laila reached the third floor landing mere seconds before her aunt and uncle stepped out of the elevator. Beads of sweat glistened on her forehead. Her face was flushed and sticky. Stopping to catch her breath, Laila slid her hand in her *abaya* pocket and pulled out an inhaler. Exhaling deeply, she drew in a long puff, held her breath for a moment, then took a second puff. Her lungs slowly relaxed, and she breathed deeper and calmer. Dr. Pettit always said she should not get too excited, as it brought on her asthma symptoms. Laila knew never to go out without her rescue inhaler.

"Laila, are you alright?" Aunt Balqees asked, her voice heavy with concern.

"Yeah, I'll be fine in a sec," Laila said, wiping her hand across her forehead. "It's hard to breathe in this heat." Her clothes were stuck to her like a second skin.

"Get some rest before we head out for *Umrah*," said Uncle Farid, stifling a yawn. "Crossing time zones is tiring. We can rest for an hour before we head out." He wheeled the luggage cart across the hallway.

"Remember to call your mo— Raisa," said Aunt Balqees, as they arrived at room number 329. "You know how she worries." She pulled out the key card and swiped it through the lock. Aunt Balqees looked at Laila, waiting for a response. Laila nodded. Her shoulders sagged, and her brow creased into a frown. Her stepmom could wait. Why would she be worried anyways?

The door buzzed as a green light lit up, and the three of them walked into the two-bedroom suite. Laila threw down her bag and kicked off her shoes. Relief flooded through her as her feet sank into the soft sand-colored carpet. Right now, all she wanted was to take off the heavy *abaya* and *hijab* and hang out in T-shirt and jeans.

The air-conditioned room felt like heaven after the humidity and heat of the outdoors. Laila pulled out her phone and took a picture of their hotel view of the Grand Mosque far in the distance, with its arches and tall minarets. She sent it to Beth with an accompanying text: "Arrived safe. Our hotel views. " Beth did not reply. It was probably too early in the morning in Chicago, Laila realized. Beth must still be sleeping.

"I can't wait to see the Kaaba," Aunt Balqees said as she poured herself a glass of water from the refrigerator. "We can head over to the mosque as soon as we get settled in."

"Sure," said Laila. "I'll be quick." She wheeled her suitcase toward her bedroom.

"Take your time," said Uncle Farid, lounging on the sofa, remote control in hand. "No hurry, we're here for a week, so relax. Get some rest." He looked very much like Baba, Laila thought, a younger version, but the resemblance and manner-isms were striking. Memories of Baba had a way of waking up and renewing her pain like an open wound.

In her room, Laila pulled open the closet and hung up her clothes. If she had come last year with Baba, things would have been different. Was she changing, Laila wondered, like Beth had said? She had been abrupt with her stepmom. She had ignored her baby sister. Only because it still hurt too much. Perhaps she should call home. Later, she decided.

Laila walked to the bed and flung herself down on it, grab-bing her phone. She saw there were two missed calls from Beth. She was up real early. Laila pressed the redial button and seconds later Beth appeared on the screen, dressed in pajamas. Her tousled brown hair framed her familiar, smiling face.

"Hey, you arrived," Beth said. "What time is it?"

"It's just past three in the afternoon," said Laila. "The flight was way too long—over twelve hours."

"Wow! You look different," said Beth. "Show me what you're wearing." Laila sprang up off the bed and placed her phone against the table lamp. She moved away to the center of the room and gave a twirl. As she spun round, the folds of her *abaya* flapped against her ankles. "Cool! You look so different, so grown up. I wouldn't recognize you if I saw you on the street."

"I feel generic," said Laila. "I look like everyone else. I guess that's kind of the point, not to stand out and draw attention."

"When do you leave for the pilgrimage? And how long will it take?" Beth asked.

"It takes a few hours I guess, because of the large crowds," said Laila.

"It sounds pretty awesome," said Beth. "Plus, you've got great weather too. We had snow again this morning."

"That's Chicago for you," said Laila. "It's absolutely boiling here. I almost melted, really, it's that hot."

"I'd love some warm weather! By the way, your stepmom called," said Beth.

"What did she want?" Laila's fists clenched as her smile vanished.

"She sounded worried, because she hasn't heard from you. Didn't you text her when you arrived?" Laila shook her head. "My mom spoke to her. You really should call her."

"Why would she call? She knows where I am," Laila said, shrugging her shoulders impatiently.

"Sure, she does, but it's just a courtesy to let her know," said Beth. "With everything going on in the world, its understandable that she wants to know you arrived safely. I mean, you live with her—she's your stepmom. It's up to you anyways..." said Beth. "Don't forget your report while you're out there having fun."

"I wouldn't call it fun exactly," said Laila. "Don't worry, I haven't forgotten my report. See you tomorrow." Both girls waved at each other, and moments later the screen went blank.

Laila threw her phone on the bed and flopped down beside it. She lay there staring at the ceiling fan. Her report could wait, but maybe she should call her stepmom. Maybe later. When they got back from the mosque.

Aunt Balqees sat, praying on a prayer mat, as Laila entered the living room. She turned her head to the right, whispering, "*Assalaamu-Alaikum-Wa-Rahmatullah.*" Then, she turned her head to the left, saying: "Peace and blessings of God be with you." Aunt Balqees then rolled the prayer mat and stood up. She turned to Laila.

"Have you prayed yet? We should be leaving soon so we can perform *Umrah* before it's time for *Asr* prayer." Laila had not prayed the second of the five daily prayers. In fact, she had not prayed one single prayer since Baba's funeral. She shook her head, unable to meet her aunt's gaze. She looked down at her feet, shifting awkwardly. "You know Laila, prayer takes practice. You must work at anything to make it effective," Aunt Balqees said gently. "Look, I don't wish to lecture you, but please don't give up on prayer. God doesn't need our prayers—we do. It helps us. It reminds us that He is looking out for us." Laila nodded and quietly sat by her aunt. She felt a twinge of guilt. Baba never missed a single prayer. She had missed too many to count.

"All set?" said Uncle Farid. "We should head out then." Laila smiled at her uncle. She couldn't get used to seeing him in *Ihram*. Her smile was bittersweet. Uncle Farid had been close to Baba. She warmed to the idea that she would perform the pilgrimage with him.

20

"The dress requirements for *Umrah* are much more lenient for women," said Aunt Balqees. "We can wear whatever we choose as long as it's simple, modest, and not ostentatious."

"I texted Raisa to let her know we arrived safe and sound, Laila," Uncle Farid said. "So, if you two are ready then let's go."

"You wait and see," Aunt Balqees whispered to Laila. "Pilgrimage will give your heart solace."

Laila walked fast, skipping down the steps ahead of her aunt and uncle. She didn't hear their conversation about her as her uncle lowered his voice in the lobby.

"Look, you can't build up her hopes. She's still a kid. How spiritual do you expect this to be for her?" He asked his wife. He saw Laila was watching the view outside the sprawling lobby windows.

"I know Farid, but she's been grieving four months now. It's too long for a kid, and she hardly smiles."

"I'm still grieving for my big brother. You can't switch it off. It takes time. Just let her be," he said, his voice was thick with emotion. "We need to be there for her. For now, that's all we can do."

CHAPTER 4
THE KAABA

Nine-year-old Laila impatiently pulled out her homework folder from her bag.

"Why do I have to learn Arabic anyways? You don't speak it Baba, so why do I need to?" asked Laila. She held out her grammar homework, looking miserable.

"I made a promise to your Mama. Arabic was her language," said Baba, "Look, I know it is hard, but trust me. You will master it—and one day, you will thank me."

Accompanied by her aunt and uncle, Laila left the cool hotel lobby. As they stepped out into the busy street, the thick afternoon heat hit them like heat from an open oven door. The air was heavy with sweet and fruity scents. They passed the vibrant vendors displaying their wares along the road as they made their way to the Grand Mosque. Fragrances of melon, papaya, and many other exotic fruits mingled with pungent perfumes. They walked briskly. As they drew closer to the Grand Mosque, the crowds grew larger and wider. Throngs of pilgrims walked in the same direction. All walked toward the Grand Mosque that housed the Kaaba—the House of God—in its central courtyard. The air was dense with people. The humidity was stifling to Laila. She patted her pocket to check her inhaler. Making sure it was there should she need it.

All men were robed in two pieces of white fabric, while women and children were dressed in an assortment of colors. It would be easy to get lost in the crowd. Laila made sure she kept close to her aunt and uncle. As they drew nearer, the road ended and they walked on marble floors, where brightly lit stores surrounded them. The massive, grand clocktower loomed above, as if touching the heavens. It seemed so different to what Laila imagined.

"Things have changed since I was here a few years ago," Aunt Balqees said, her voice filled with regret. "Here we are in the holiest place on earth, surrounded by designer stores." She sighed as Laila took in all the sights and sounds. If there had not been pilgrims walking beside them, they could easily have been in any shopping mall.

Laila slipped off her shoes outside the entrance to the Grand Mosque. She followed her aunt and uncle as they made their way through the doorway, the *Baab,* and through arches leading to marble stairs.

"I'm thirsty," said Laila. Her throat suddenly felt dry, her lips parched.

"We can drink water from the well of Zamzam," said Uncle Farid. "It has been here for thousands of years. Pilgrims have been drinking from this well since Abraham first built the Kaaba." They each took a cup of cool water. It tasted different but felt refreshing in the afternoon heat. Laila wondered how it must have felt when baby Ishmael and his mother Hagar first drank from the well.

They made their way downstairs. Laila felt nervous.

"What do I do? What do I say?" she asked.

"Remember to say a special prayer when you see the Kaaba for the first time," Uncle Farid said. "Whatever you pray for will be granted to you."

"Just pray with your heart, in your own language," said Aunt Balqees gently.

Laila jostled shoulder to shoulder with pilgrims making their way to the Kaaba. What would she pray for? She knew what she wanted was impossible. She could never get her life with Baba back. Baba had talked of this moment many times. He had talked of taking her to the Holy Kaaba. If it hadn't been for Naila, they would have come here together.

Baba had told her how the Kaaba was first built by Adam, as the first place on earth where the One God was worshipped. Centuries later, Abraham rebuilt it with his son Ishmael. Now Laila was here. She was about to face it. Her heart beat a little faster. Her hands were clammy. The marble beneath her bare feet was cool.

A sudden hush descended upon the crowd. Goosebumps crawled up Laila's arms and down her neck, as the late afternoon sun burned down on her head.

She had seen the Kaaba in pictures, but up close it was bigger; familiar, yet utterly strange. She stood in awe, wondering what to pray. The black cube stood forty feet high, draped in black jacquard fabric, covered with intricate and ornate gold embroidery. Its raised, ornate door was closed shut. Opened only for special occasions.

Pilgrims wept. A grown man sobbed as he prayed. The emotional surge was a strong force all around Laila. It was powerful. Palpable. Here she was. She stood there, staring up at this cube, a place of worship since time immemorial. She waited to feel something. She felt numb. What were they feeling, she wondered? And why did she feel nothing? Here she was, at the House of God, where people all around her prayed earnestly. She felt nothing but the heavy lump of grief that had lodged itself in her heart when her father died.

Laila pushed through the crowds of pilgrims, keeping close to her aunt and uncle. An elbow dug into her ribs as a tall woman in black pushed past her. She had to keep moving fast. A group of women linking arms together moved swiftly, pushing everyone out of the way. Her *abaya* grew heavier and stickier as the late afternoon sun burned down on her covered head.

"There are so many people, I don't know what to do," she whispered as she clung to her aunt. Her feet shuffled smoothly across the marble floor as she walked with pilgrims, some old, some young, some carrying children on their shoulders, while the elderly were wheeled around in wheelchairs.

Laila followed the pilgrims, as they flocked around the Kaaba in a sea of movement, counterclockwise. Around them were rows upon rows of marble arches that stood across smooth marble floors. People traveled there from across the globe, like a united humanity.

Her whole life, Baba had talked of visiting here. Now here she was. And Baba was not.

"We must first perform the *Tawaf* by going around the Kaaba seven times," Uncle Farid told Laila. "We begin at the black stone, then go counterclockwise. Stay close to me and your aunt. If we get separated, then we should meet up at the Station of Abraham." Uncle Farid pointed to the gold hexagon-shaped structure facing opposite the door of the Kaaba. It was an easy landmark. Laila was relieved. It was a large structure, easy to find amidst the crowds. "It contains the footprints of Abraham set in rock."

"Laila," Aunt Balqees gently touched her arm. "Remember to pray with your heart. God listens. He has invited you to His house. We are all here at His invitation."

Laila nodded, wondering if she had a heart and why she

felt nothing. She whispered prayers she had learned by heart as a child, but they were mere words. She walked in the heat, sliding her feet as she moved with the flow of the tide. She wanted it to mean something. She had waited for this moment so long. She went through the rituals, trying to grasp something meaningful, trying to hold onto her faith, which she feared was slipping away. She counted each round she made as she completed each circumambulation. To her right, a group of women pushed past her. They were all dressed in black. The leader of their group held a sign above them.

A smart way to keep everyone together, Laila observed, as she continued moving forward. She almost lost sight of her aunt and uncle, when another group linking arms together nudged her side. Some pushed through the crowd, elbowing anyone who came into their path. Laila winced as she felt an elbow dig her in the ribs. She was certain that would leave a bruise.

The moving crowd was like a flowing river. Everyone seemed determined to reach and touch the Black Stone. It became a turbulent vortex of people, and Laila felt herself get sucked in, unable to pull away, she let herself go with the flow.

Each *Tawaf* around the Kaaba took longer as Laila felt herself moving further away from the Kaaba. If she were closer to the Kaaba, the circuit would be shorter. She tried to move closer, but each try took her further away. On her seventh round, Laila lost sight of her aunt and uncle. She was pulled with the crowd, now going closer to the Kaaba. She came near enough to touch the Kaaba. The wind whipped soft ripples through the black fabric that covered the stone structure. Laila felt the gentle vibrations as the wind rustled through the fabric. It seemed that time stood still. Laila saw the Black Stone, *Hajar-al-Aswad,* framed in silver.

Laila reached out to touch the Black Stone. Hard and

smooth, it was cool to the touch. This was the same stone Abraham was given by Angel Gabriel; the same stone that withstood the passage of time; touched by millions of pilgrims over thousands of years. Laila's heart beat fast. Her hands shook as her fingers slid over the cool stone. From the deepest depths within her soul, where pain had lodged itself, a prayer rose from her heart. *Help me. Help make the pain go away. Help me understand.*

Laila felt light headed from the glaring heat of the afternoon sun. She shifted her feet on the marble as a wave of dizziness washed over her. She stumbled and suddenly feeling queasy, she put her hand to her forehead. The pilgrims around her seemed to blend together. They blurred and became a sea of white, swimming around a black cube. Everything slowed down and became out-of-focus. It felt as if Laila was watching a slow-motion movie. She felt she was in a trance, when suddenly she became acutely aware that her feet were burning. She felt as if she stood on hot coals.

The marble floor had vanished and was replaced by sand. The steady hum of pilgrims was gone, replaced by a curious and eerie quiet. They had simply vanished, as if erased by an invisible hand.

CHAPTER 5
LOST IN TIME

Laila waited as Baba stood in prayer. She watched his movements; as he bowed his forehead touching the ground. She could not hear what he quietly said. When he finished praying, he rolled up his rug and looked at her.

"Why do you pray five times a day?" asked Laila.

"It's a reminder to be mindful of our Creator," said Baba. "We have to stop whatever we're doing and connect in prayer."

"But how does it help?" asked Laila.

"When you stand before your Creator, then everything falls into place. You feel like a small atom in the vast universe. You feel your place in all creation, for everything is connected, and you find peace."

LAILA GASPED AS SHE TOOK IN HER SURROUNDINGS. THE towering buildings that surrounded the Grand Mosque were gone. They were replaced by hills. Laila looked all around frantically, holding her hand to her forehead. Her aunt and uncle had disappeared along with the thousands of pilgrims. A stone structure stood before her, but it was different. It was in the same place the Kaaba had stood moments before. It was a cubed, stone structure, with a green-striped cover. There were two doors in it, and one stood wide open. Two men dressed in long robes walked through the doors. It was the Kaaba—the one constant in a transformed reality—but it looked different. Everything was different. The large skyscrapers that loomed beyond were gone.

Laila's limbs trembled. The glare of the sun blinded her. She shaded her eyes with the back of her hand. Panic rose within her. Her heartbeat quickened as fear rippled through her. She closed her eyes and took deep breaths to calm her shaking.

She pulled herself together and looked around, hoping no one noticed her. She edged forward, and what she saw made her heart beat faster. Through the doors of the Kaaba, she saw rows of stone shaped carvings, in different shapes and sizes. They were statues made of stone and wooden carvings inside the Kaaba. She shook her head. *That is impossible*, she told herself as she clasped her arms around her. She must be dreaming, she decided, for she knew from history that the last time the Kaaba had statues in it was over fourteen hundred years ago. Her head ached. Her throat was parched. She felt faint.

Laila moved away from the Kaaba and took in her surroundings. The Kaaba was the largest building there, in a valley surrounded by hills. Smaller buildings stood in the distance. The weight of her *abaya* grew heavier. She felt as if it stuck to her like glue. The climate was sticky, with odors hanging heavy in the air. It was hot and smelly. Laila wrinkled her nose and lifted the corner of her *hijab* to cover her face. The sun's heat was fierce as it blazed down. People walked by and stared at her. Shepherds herded goats on distant hills. Riders rode on the backs of camels. Donkeys brayed, complaining of heavy loads on their backs. A horse grazed languidly as it stood tethered to a palm tree. A man sat on the dirt road and sold milk from a pail to passersby. Pungent smells reminded Laila of the indoor animal house at Brook-field Zoo. She felt faint from the heat, smells and lack of water.

Laila knew she had to get away somewhere, away from all the stares. First, she needed water or she would pass out. *Zamzam!* Laila remembered the well of *Zamzam* was thousands of years old. She knew pilgrims to the Kaaba had been drinking the spring water since Abraham's time. She needed to find it.

She turned and looked around for the well. She felt a tightness in her lungs and reached into her pocket for her inhaler. She was being watched and shifted uncomfortably, looking around.

Alone and afraid, Laila wondered how she would get back to her aunt and uncle—her own world, wherever that was. Then she saw the well. A girl about her age stood at the well as she filled a leather pouch with water. She wore a dust-covered robe; her long black hair was braided. She turned, as if sensing Laila's gaze, and their eyes met. Laila breathed a sigh of relief as the girl approached her. She smiled at Laila and held out the leather pouch. Laila reached out gratefully. Cupping her hands together, she caught the pouring water to slake her thirst. When she had her fill, she wiped her mouth and smiled at the girl.

"*Shukran,*" Laila said, thanking the girl who smiled and nodded in return. She reached out and touched Laila's *abaya*.

"This fabric is so fine. You must be from the north. Are you with the caravan from Syria?" she asked.

"I come from much farther," said Laila. "My mother was from Syria. She died when I was two. I'm Laila." She didn't know why she gave so much information to a stranger, but for some strange reason she felt safe with this girl.

"I'm Zaynab. Come with me. You are a stranger here, and

people are staring," Zaynab said. "My mother is waiting for me. You are welcome to have a meal with us before you rejoin your caravan." Laila looked around. She decided to follow Zaynab as the watchful eyes of strangers was unsettling.

The two girls made their way past peddlers and merchants on the dirt road as they headed to the hills. A man rode on a donkey half his size, yelling and whipping him for being slow. Laila gasped and clenched her fists as her heart went out to the poor donkey. She yelled out at the man; her voice shook with anger. Zaynab took her arm and moved her away, as the man shook his fist at them.

"Mind your place woman!" he yelled.

"And what place might that be?" Laila yelled back angrily. A crowd gathered around them, curious to see the goings on.

"Hush, Laila. You can't do that here," Zaynab said. "You are a stranger here—and a girl."

"What has me being a girl got to do with calling out injustice when I see it?" Laila said as her face puckered into a frown.

"You do not know what conditions are like here. Do not put us in danger by your recklessness. I have no father to protect me and my mother. You make it difficult for us if you do not stay quiet. Invisible."

"I'm sorry," Laila said, visibly shaken. Where was she, that she needed to be invisible for her own safety? What kind of place, or alternate reality had she come to?

"Girls aren't valued here. There is much injustice." Zaynab said, with a deep sigh. Her gray eyes clouded. "There is one man who speaks of justice for women... so I hold onto hope."

They arrived at a cluster of huts on a hill and entered a tiny hut. Laila thought it was about the size of her kitchen. It was the only room in the hut. A mattress of woven date palms lay spread on the ground. A woman lay on it, with a small bundle beside her.

"This is my mother," Zaynab said. She kneeled on the ground and kissed her mother tenderly. She poured water from the leather pouch into a copper cup, and helped her mother up, supporting her as she drank. The drink revived her mother. She sat up and stared at Laila, a curious look appeared in her gray eyes.

"Omie, this is Laila," Zaynab said. "She has come to help us just like you said. You do not have to worry anymore. Your prayers have been answered." Laila looked from Zaynab to her mother, wondering what she meant. Omie looked at Laila, her gray eyes piercing. Laila shifted uncomfortably, wondering what was going on.

The baby, wrapped in a blanket of goat's hair awoke. Her eyes crinkled into raisins as she let out a piercing cry. A chill tingled down Laila's spine. Goosebumps made the hairs on her neck stand on end. In the heat of the airless room, Laila shivered. It was the cry she had heard many times in her dreams.

CHAPTER 6
ZAYNAB'S SISTER

Four-year-old Laila rolled out her prayer mat.

"I'm going to pray, Baba," she said with a determined look.

"What will you pray for?" Baba asked.

*"I'm going to ask why God took Mama away. We still need her,"
said Laila, "don't we Baba?"*

"This is my baby sister. She's barely two weeks old,"
said Zaynab. "Her life is in danger." Zaynab looked at Laila as
her lips quivered. She braced her arms together as she continued. "We need to leave Mecca as soon as possible. We must
go to the city of Yathrib. She will be safe there."

"You came to help us," Omie said. She looked at Laila
with a sad smile. "I knew help would come. You are here to
help." Laila looked at Omie, then at Zaynab. She wondered,
had they gone crazy, or was she losing her mind?

"How can I possibly help?" Laila said, as she nervously
clasped her hands together. "I mean, I'm not even from
around here." She rubbed her neck, suddenly feeling stifled in
the heat of the humid room. "I need to get home. I'm sorry,

but I really can't help you." Laila felt sick to her stomach, and guilty. They looked so helpless and were relying on her. She needed to get back to her aunt and uncle; that was the priority.

"Omie had these dreams," said Zaynab. "She dreamed a girl would save my baby sister. She told me a girl would come from far away, from another world. When I saw you, I remembered Omie's premonition." Zaynab's voice had a tone of desperation that Laila could not ignore. Zaynab's voice was low as her eyes filled with tears. She brushed them away, glancing at Omie who was now nursing the baby.

"My father died four weeks ago," Zaynab continued. Her voice was husky as she choked back her tears. "My uncle took us in. He also took ownership of all the camels my father owned. At first, he was kind, but he was waiting for a boy, whom he would raise as his own. When my sister was born, he was furious. He blamed Omie and treated us both badly."

"But why?" Laila asked. She was confused.

"A fatherless girl is a burden here, while boys are valued as prized possessions. Boys bring wealth," said Zaynab. Laila gasped in horror at what she was hearing. "Men want sons to help them when they grow up. For them, girls are a burden." Zaynab's voice was harsh with frustration. "It may not be like that where you come from. But I saw the way my uncle looked at my sister whenever she cried. I'm afraid for her safety every moment that we remain here in Mecca."

"B-but how can it be?" Laila asked in a whisper, feeling a mixture of horror and incredulity.

"I have seen baby girls disappear from families. There are whispers. Then one day the baby is gone. They become a distant memory. Forgotten just as the wind blows away footprints in the sand." Zaynab's voice faltered many times. "Since my father died, we feel alone and helpless." Laila felt for Zaynab. She knew loss. It was like a hole inside that pulled you into darkness. And from that deep-dark hole, it was difficult to climb out.

"I'm sorry," said Laila. She needed to figure out where she was and how to get back to her aunt and uncle. "Where is your uncle now?"

"He is away on business. But we cannot wait. We must leave before he returns. We must leave soon." Zaynab said, urgently appealing for Laila's help.

"What will happen if you stay here?" Laila asked.

"People bury their unwanted daughters alive!" Zaynab cried. "You must understand, we cannot remain here." Laila shivered as Zaynab's words sank in. This was Zaynab's world. It was a terrible reality she had to face. She looked to Laila for help. Laila did not know how she would help.

"But how?" Laila said. "How can I help?"

"There is a Messenger who speaks out against injustice. Some say he is the Messenger of God. He speaks of equality for women. He speaks up against these bad practices of our society," Zaynab said. "Omie says he is truthful, and we should go where he is."

"And this Messenger you speak of," said Laila, "where can we find him? How can he help?"

"He was forced out of Mecca because he stood for truth and supported the helpless. He was forced to leave Mecca when his life was threatened. He left for Yathrib, and now there is a whole community there. That is where we must go. That is where we will find peace, safety, and justice."

Yathrib! Goosebumps crept up Laila's arms. She knew the city's name from history. She was figuring out where she was, yet she thought it was impossible.

"If Omie and I go with the baby to Yathrib, she will be safe. We will have the chance to begin a new life there," Zaynab said. "We believe in the Messenger. Omie says he speaks the truth, and people do not want to hear the truth because they don't wish to change their lifestyle. They reject truth for its inconvenience."

"So, the Messenger you speak of – you believe he is the Messenger of God?" Laila asked. Zaynab nodded. Laila's voice quivered, as the reality sank in and she realized the truth.

She whispered, "I'm in the time of the Prophet of Islam, in seventh century Arabia!"

CHAPTER 7
THE SEVENTH CENTURY

On a sandy beach one summer's day, Baba and 6-year-old Laila made sandcastles. Laila picked up a dead crab. "Look Baba, it's not moving. Is it dead?"

"I'm afraid it is, Beti." Baba said.

"Baba, what if you die?" Laila asked.

"See this shell," said Baba, picking up a conch shell from the sand. "Once there was a creature that lived in it. It has gone now, but the shell remains. When we die, we leave our bodies. Our souls live on when we leave our bodies."

"Will you leave me?" asked Laila.

"I will never leave you," said Baba.

Laila knew the history. Baba had taught her well. The Messenger of God was persecuted for his beliefs, so he migrated to the city of Yathrib, later renamed Medina. Seventh century Arabia, known as the *Hejaz*, was a place of much injustice known as the period of *Jahiliah*, the time of ignorance. *The Messenger of God came as an emancipator when Arabia was in the depths of darkness. He came as a light of reason, as*

37

a liberator. Baba often told Laila this when she would question him about Islam; when she had doubts in her mind brought on by questions raised in the media and around her. Did this mean she would meet the Messenger if they traveled to Yathrib? She gasped with nervous excitement. There was a possibility of meeting the one person Baba revered more than any other human being on Earth. Perhaps this was her chance to find her faith? Perhaps this was why she came to be here.

"Why can't you simply go and join the Messenger in the city of Yathrib?" Laila said.

"It is too dangerous. A long and hazardous journey by caravan, through a treacherous desert. You must help us join your caravan," Zaynab said. "We are two women with a baby, unaccompanied by a man. With your help, we can join you when your caravan returns to Syria." Laila suddenly realized why they were counting on her, and she shook her head.

"I'm sorry. I can't help you," she said, and her heart sank. If she went with them to Yathrib, she would meet the Messenger and they would be safe. Her head hung low as she rubbed the back of her neck. "Is there another caravan you can join? I'm sorry, I don't belong to a caravan," said Laila, with a deep sigh. She was disappointed she could not help them, even more so that she would not meet the Messenger.

"Where did you come from? Did you not come in a caravan?" Zaynab asked.

"You are from another world," Omie said. "I know you came to help us."

"Surely you can join another caravan," Laila insisted, hoping fervently they could still find a way to reach the safety of Yathrib.

"Since the Messenger left Mecca, the Meccan chiefs are angry. They have placed an embargo on all trade to Yathrib," Zaynab said sadly. "No one would be willing to risk their lives and livelihood, even if we did join a caravan. We need someone who knows us. Someone who would be willing to take a detour when we cross the desert."

"First we must eat. Do not worry, we will find a way," Omie said. "Please join us, as our guest." The baby lay, peacefully sleeping, unaware of the anxiety that filled the hut, nor aware of the danger to her life.

Sitting together cross-legged on the ground, Laila shared a meal of bread and milk with Zaynab and Omie. She realized how hungry she was as she bit into the soft buttered bread. The goat's milk was cold and sweet. It soothed her throat and she felt refreshed after the simple meal. Laila determined she would find a way to get them to Yathrib—and a way she could meet the Messenger.

"So, when do the caravans leave?" Laila asked, as she bit into a juicy date that Zaynab offered. "Is there anyone you know who would not mind a few more passengers?"

"My late husband's friend has a caravan that comes and goes frequently. He is a merchant and travels with goods from the north," Omie said, her voice soft and hopeful.

"Can we ask him?" Laila asked. "Would he mind carrying more passengers?"

"If we had a man with us, there would be no problem," Zaynab said, with a disappointed sigh. "He wouldn't want to anger the other members of the caravan. They travel together to avoid attacks by marauders." Laila stood up impatiently, brushing crumbs off her *abaya*. There simply had to be a way. She paced up and down the small room. Zaynab picked up the sheet from the ground and shook the crumbs. Her head was downcast as she looked at Omie.

"Don't worry Zaynab," Omie said with a sad smile. She bent over the baby and picked her up. "We must not lose hope." Though her eyes looked deep with despair, and her thin face looked devoid of hope.

"We must find a way," Laila whispered out loud as she

shook her head in frustration. She felt there had to be a reason she was there. She racked her brains, trying to come up with a solution. She pulled off her *hijab* and shook out her long, black hair. The heat was getting to her. She wondered what she should do to solve their man-less situation. Laila's face suddenly broke into a wide smile. A gleam appeared in her eyes as an idea hatched in her head. *She could do this. She would do this!*

"Do you have scissors?" Laila asked suddenly as she looked about the room.

"Scissors?" Zaynab repeated. "What do you mean? What for?" She looked at Laila, her face confused.

"You know," Laila said quickly. "I mean, whatever do you use to cut hair?" She motioned with her hands. Zaynab went to a wooden chest in the corner of the room. She took out a metal contraption that Laila could have sworn she saw in some ancient Babylonian exhibit on her last trip to the museum. This piece of antiquity was what they used as scissors! Laila gasped as she took the flat metal shears. She smoothed her hand over her silky, long, black hair, then pulled a handful of it in a bunch. *Snip! Snip! Snip!* Her hair fell softly to the ground in chunks with each snip of the shears. As the silky, black locks of hair fell to the ground, it drew gasps of horror from Omie and Zaynab.

"What are you doing?" said Zaynab, her face horror stricken.

"Hair is a woman's beauty," Omie whispered. "Why are you cutting it?"

"If I'm here to help you, then this is what I must do," Laila said, appearing braver than she felt. She looked at her reflection in a polished brass plate and smiled. "Not bad for a do-it-yourself hairdo. Not great either, but it'll do." Laila brushed the uneven edges of her almost-pixie-cut hair style. Next, she took the ends of her *hijab,* opened it out into a square, then twisted it into a rope. She wound the rope-like fabric around her head into a turban, then spun round to face Zaynab and Omie.

"Meet your cousin!" Laila said.

"You look like a boy!" said Omie, stammering with incredulity. "You take such a risk for us. May God bless you always." Omie hugged Laila warmly. As she moved away, the folds of her shawl moved to reveal a pendant hanging around her neck. Laila stared at it, wondering why it looked familiar. She shook her head, telling herself that her mind was playing tricks on her.

"I can give you my father's robes to help your disguise," Zaynab said. Laila tucked her *abaya* in the belt of her jeans, then covered herself with a coarse robe that belonged to Zaynab's father.

"Don't worry, layers make you cooler in the desert heat," said Zaynab.

Now came the difficult part. Laila had taken on the insurmountable responsibility of getting the baby to safety. Zaynab and Omie had faith in her, more so than she herself. How she would manage to cross the desert to Yathrib, she had no idea. Like Omie, she too would need to take a leap of faith.

CHAPTER 8
THE CARAVAN

"Laila," said Baba as he held out a small bundle. "Meet your sister." Laila felt a mixture of wonder and curiosity. She had never held a baby, and this tiny bundle was her sister, barely a few hours old. Laila looked at her eyes, brown, almond shaped, with thick black eyelashes. Her tiny arms were as small as Laila's middle finger. She smiled at her sister and her stepmom, who sat in the hospital bed watching Laila, waiting for her response.

"Welcome to our family, little sis," she whispered with a smile.

At sunset, Laila followed Zaynab out to the campsite. The evening air blew a cool breeze softly across the desert sand as the two girls made their way down the hill, toward the valley. Groups of people loaded camels with crates, boxes, and sacks of merchandise as they prepared for their trade route bound for Syria.

"Mecca is the center for traders from the north and the south," Zaynab said. They slowed their footsteps and stood to watch the busy merchants. Zaynab and Laila looked very much like a girl and boy as they watched and waited for a familiar face. The disguise worked, as to any observer they were brother and sister.

"What if he's not here?" Laila asked. She felt strange in an unfamiliar place, amidst a crowd of strangers. "We have to find them," she whispered, as the heat felt heavy, like her heart.

"Don't worry, we will find him. I played with his son, Khalil, as a child. His father is a good man," Zaynab said.

"Are they from here?" Laila asked.

"Yes, but they have always been traders, like nomads, always traveling. Since Khalil turned fifteen, he always accompanies his father. It has been some time since I saw him," Zaynab said. She smiled suddenly as she spotted a familiar face. She walked over to a tall young man. He looked up when she called his name, and smiled warmly at Zaynab. Laila watched their interaction from a distance.

"How are you, Khalil?" Zaynab said.

"Greetings Zaynab, I am well. And you, how have you been?" he asked. "It has been too long." Standing a head taller than Zaynab, Khalil was dressed in long, layered robes, with a turban on his head and a sword in a scabbard tied around his waist.

"It's good to see you, Khalil," Zaynab said. "Are you and your father keeping well?"

"Busy as ever," Khalil replied. "We are on the go, always traveling back and forth." Khalil placed his hand on his heart. "I was sorry to hear of your father. We were away when we heard the sad news of his passing." Zaynab's eyes clouded for a moment. She lowered her head to compose herself.

"Thank you," she said. "It was sudden. A great shock for us." Zaynab turned to Laila, "I want you to meet my cousin Lai—Layth." Laila held her breath as she waited for her disguise to fall through. Her heart pounded in her ribs. She was certain everyone could hear it, and sure her disguise was up.

Khalil's black eyes had a glint in them as he greeted Laila, taking her hand firmly in his. His handshake was strong; his smile was warm and trusting. Laila was glad the darkness hid her face, which suddenly grew warm. She felt guilty and afraid of the pretense. It's for a worthy cause, she reminded herself. *In life-threatening danger, it's okay to bend the rules.* But being deceitful did not feel good, nor right.

"Khalil, can you and your father make room for another family in your caravan?" Zaynab asked as she explained their situation. "We are ready to leave as soon as you wish."

Khalil was happy to help, but first he had to consult his father, Abi. Zaynab and Laila waited with baited breath as Khalil went over to a group of merchants deep in discussion. He touched his father's shoulder, who turned to Khalil. His face looked much like an older version of Khalil, Laila thought as she watched the father and son talk quietly for some time. There was a frown on Abi's face. Laila's heart sank. Would this be the end of everything? Would she be unable to see the Messenger of God and save the baby's life? Would she ever get home?

Khalil turned and walked back over to where the two girls stood. Seeing the smile on his face, both Laila and Zaynab sighed with relief. "Abi is happy to help his friend's family," Khalil told them. "We are leaving as soon as the camels are loaded and fed. It's safer to travel by night."

Abi joined their group. He wore a long *thobe,* like Khalil, with a large turban on his head. He stood tall like his son, though he was of a wider and stockier build. He greeted Zaynab with his hand on his heart as he offered his condolences for her loss. He turned to Laila with a smile, and warmly shook her hand.

"Layth. Welcome, young man. Any relative of my dear

friend is welcome," said Abi. "As you can see we are very busy here. Mecca is a busy import and export city. Many caravans arrive with goods, while others are preparing to leave. One caravan arrived last night with incense from the south. We brought fabric and leather from the north. Now we make ready to leave again."

"It is always good to be back, even for only two nights at a time," said Khalil. "This will always be home to me. It has changed much since I was a child and is now the central hub of the world."

The hustle and bustle continued as the caravan of two hundred camels, together with some horses and goats, prepared to begin their journey across the desert. Merchants loaded their valuable wares on the camels' backs, hoping for profit in distant lands.

"We will sit in the *Shuqduf*," said Zaynab. She pointed to an enclosed mini-carriage on top of the camel. "You must ride with the men." Laila realized this was not going to be easy.

The *Shuqduf* was hoisted up to seat Omie, Zaynab, and the baby. It had cushioned seats with coverings of soft goat's hair. Laila breathed nervously. She would have to ride a camel by herself. She reminded herself that she had to act like a boy. Each traveler was too busy to notice the three new passengers and a baby when they joined the caravan with Abi and Khalil.

When Zaynab told Omie that they were to leave at sundown, she quickly gathered everything she owned and packed it in a small rucksack. All they brought was a leather pouch of water, a bag of dates, and a pot of yogurt. Omie breathed a sigh of relief. She was leaving her old life, which was no longer safe for her baby. She said a quiet prayer for protection as Laila turned to her camel. Omie said, "I pray to the Almighty, not to the idols that others worship. The Almighty will guide us to safety." Omie said it with a surety Laila wished she could feel.

Laila climbed on the seated camel and gripped the reins. Slowly, her camel stood up to its tall height, swaying from side to side. She sat tall, astride the camel, and her heart beat fast. Khalil rode beside her, and Abi rode on ahead. The *Shuqduf* was right in front of them. Laila lurched forward as the camel took long and wobbly strides. She felt like she was on the sea as her seat moved with the rhythmic rocking motion of the camel. *Maybe that's why they're known as ships of the desert*, Laila mused. Omie and Zaynab peered out from the *Shuqduf* opening to see that she was fine. Laila was glad she had taken horse-riding lessons, though the camel was far bumpier than riding a horse.

There was a rumbling of movement as the caravan embarked on what would be a long and arduous journey. They were at the rear of the caravan as it set off. The thudding and plodding of camels' hooves kicked up clouds of dust. Stars blanketed the night sky, and a soft breeze blew, warm as a whisper. With moonlight to guide them, the travelers continued onward. Laila was quiet as she listened to the hoof-beats of her camel, synchronized with her heartbeat. She wondered if she would ever get home. She thought of her stepmom and Naila and decided that if she ever got home, she would be kinder than she had been since Baba died—and more attentive to Naila. After all, she was her sister.

"Layth? Are you asleep?" Khalil asked. Laila did not answer. "Layth!"

"No—um, yes, I'm awake," Laila said, when she suddenly realized he was speaking to her.

"Don't fall asleep while riding a camel. You will slip off and no one will notice until you are left behind in the desert. It will be too late to turn back," Khalil said. Laila studied his face and could not tell if he was joking. His face was serious. She shuddered at the thought of being left alone in the barren, rocky, vast expanse of emptiness.

"So how do you plan to go to Yathrib if this caravan is headed for Syria?" Laila asked. She lowered her voice, hoping it sounded deep.

"It will be tricky to change our route to Yathrib," Khalil said. "As everyone knows, Meccans have forbidden trade with Yathrib since the Messenger left Mecca. He received an enthusiastic welcome from the people of Yathrib. He has growing support there and the Meccans are angry. They have banned all trade with Yathrib. Don't worry, we will find a way. That is the reason we are at the rear of the caravan. It will be easier for you to break off and head in another direction when the time comes. There is no need to worry about that yet. First we have to survive the five-day journey before we are faced with that situation."

"What do you mean survive?" Laila asked. Khalil laughed.

"Have you never journeyed through the desert?" Khalil looked surprised. Laila shook her head. There was no need to pretend. "We could be robbed. We could die in a sandstorm or run out of water. There are many ways to die in a desert." Khalil said, enjoying the look of fear on Laila's face. Laila took a deep breath and tried to think of things, ordinary things, like her school report that was due next week. Somehow it did not seem important right now. It was not due for another fourteen centuries. Laila almost smiled at the thought, but there was too much uncertainty to feel anything but fear. A fear that curled into a tight ball in the pit of her stomach.

"Oh, and I forgot to mention scorpions," said Khalil. "One bite could be lethal." Laila shuddered. This was going to be one long ride.

CHAPTER 9
THE JOURNEY

"Life is like a puzzle," said Baba, *"We are all trying to figure out where we fit in, where we belong. But if we step back and see the bigger picture, we'll see that we're all connected. We're all part of this huge puzzle of creation. And it's beautiful. It can leave you breathless with wonder. Just think of the Author of all this—this beautiful universe. How can we not worship the One who created us?"*

Morning dawned with a blazing orange sunrise, mixed with pink and purple hues. The sky was a canvas of color that lit up the sand. It shimmered in the dappled, golden light. The weary travelers found a place to rest, just as the desert temperatures rose, from the coolness of the night to the blazing heat of day. Laila covered her face with the end of her turban as the sun's heat burned down. It helped disguise her in the bright daylight.

The head of the caravan came to a stop. Others slowly followed. The travelers dismounted and prepared for their daytime rest. Both animals and humans were ready for replenishment of food and drink after a long trek through the night.

Khalil coaxed his camel into sitting on the ground. He then slid off effortlessly, his sandaled feet sank in a soft thud on the sand. Laila's camel followed suit, and she too disembarked. Relief flooded through her aching muscles. Her body was stiff, tired, and aching all over.

"It's good to feel the ground under my feet," Laila said with feeling as she stretched her tired muscles. Khalil stepped forward to assist with Zaynab and Omie's camel. He took the reins and guided the camel to sit. The camel's large body wobbled as he maneuvered himself into sitting comfortably on the ground. Laila and Khalil both reached out to grab hold of Zaynab and Omie as they climbed safely out of the *Shuq-duf*. The baby slept on, unaware of all the commotion. Laila was reminded of Naila when she saw the small bundle in Omie's arms. A twinge of regret tugged her heart. Naila was once that small, but Laila had been too absorbed in herself to notice or care. She wondered sadly if she would have a second chance with her baby sister. She feared she may never see her again. Her heart lurched as questions crowded her mind.

Laila turned to her camel. She had grown fond of his gentle nature. She patted his side. "You need a name," she whispered softly. "Jemel is a good name. It means camel in Arabic, so I think it suits you. Thank you for being so patient, Jemel, you deserve a drink first."

"Don't worry, he can go without water for several days," said Khalil. "Camels are very resilient. They don't feel thirst like we do."

The horses and goats were fed. The camels were content with dried leaves and brush. After eating, the animals quietly snoozed beneath the shade of palm trees. The oasis had become an instant town as hundreds of travelers set up camp. The place bustled with activity. A steady hum of conversation filled the usually quiet desert. Each group gathered their belongings and began setting up tents. Laila helped Khalil and Abi set up their makeshift tents. Though it was a struggle for her, they didn't seem to mind her awkwardness and lack of knowledge.

"I can see you are new to this," Khalil said with a friendly grin. "Don't worry, when I first joined my father a few summers ago, it took me a while to learn. That's how it is." He shrugged his shoulders and patted Laila's back. Laila was impressed how within minutes the tent was up, with four poles dug into the sand and an animal hide hung over to shelter them from the sun. Rows upon rows of tents soon stood in the clearing. Tired and hungry, they sat down to eat. Khalil, Laila, Abi, Omie, and Zaynab shared a meal of bread and dates, accompanied by fresh goat milk. After clearing up the food utensils, they prepared for rest.

"We will rest a while, then continue at sundown," Abi said. "It is fortunate that the sky is clear. A sandstorm would be a disaster and delay our journey. We must be watchful, for there are brigands roaming the desert, always ready to prey on unsuspecting travelers."

"Would they attack our caravan?" Laila asked, feeling nervous at the thought of yet more dangers to face.

"Usually, such a large caravan should be safe, but you never know. We must be ever vigilant," Abi said. "A traveler is never safe until he reaches his destination. I have been a merchant all my life and have seen what people are capable of doing for greed." Laila sighed and hoped fervently they would be safe.

"We always come prepared," Khalil said, patting his sword in its sheath. Laila shuddered but said nothing. She could not tell them that she hated any kind of weapon. She was horrified to see every male traveler carrying a weapon, but then she told herself: *This is a different world. This is the time of the*

Jahiliyah, the time before the Messenger of God brought about change for good.

As the travelers rested, the sun rose high in the heavens. Abi and Khalil shared a tent. Zaynab was in another tent with Omie and the baby. Laila looked around awkwardly. She shifted her feet nervously, clenching her hands. What was she supposed to do? She wondered where she would sleep. Thankfully, Zaynab saved the day.

"Layth, can you set your tent beside ours?" Zaynab said aloud, purposefully so Khalil and Abi would hear her. "Omie feels very nervous, especially since my father died. She will feel relieved to know you are close by."

"That should not be a problem," said Khalil, unperturbed. "It only takes a minute to replant a tent." Zaynab breathed a shaky sigh of relief and Laila's pounding heart quieted. A few moments later, Laila's tent was moved from the men's area, closer to Omie and Zaynab's tent. Laila breathed a sigh of relief as Omie patted Khalil's head tenderly. He bowed his head in respect.

Omie, Zaynab, and the baby settled down, and soon there was silence in their tent. Sleep evaded Laila. Thoughts of home crowded her mind as she lay on her makeshift bed on the rough ground. Eventually, the hum around the campsite lulled to a quiet peacefulness as slumber descended all around. Laila, too, fell into an exhausted and dreamless sleep.

She awoke several hours later, when the sun was sinking lower toward the horizon. She was surprised at how soundly she had slept on the hard ground, with only a piece of animal hide for bedding. Laila joined Khalil, Abi, Zaynab, and Omie for a meal of yoghurt, bread, and dates. They sat beneath the shade of a palm tree, waiting for the evening, watching as the sun sank.

The descending sun appeared a burning, blood red orb as it sank beneath the golden horizon. The desert fell into darkness. Rest was at an end. The cover of darkness meant safety for the travelers, and the evening cooled to a pleasant temperature. The travelers packed up their tents and belongings. They reloaded the camels' backs with their heavy burdens to carry onward.

As if on cue, stars lit up the darkening sky while the radiant moon illuminated their path. The gentle plodding of the camels' hooves continued as they lumbered on, heavy with their loads as ships of the desert. Their heavy breathing, interspersed with the trudging of their footsteps, resounded across the otherwise silent desert.

It was a long and uneventful night. Laila heard sounds from the *Shuqduf* ahead as Zaynab and Omie consoled the restless baby.

"It is hard for the baby," said Khalil. "More so though, for the mother." The baby's cries grew louder.

"Yes," Laila said. "The poor baby is so restless tonight." She grew curious. "Where is your mother, Khalil? What is your story?"

"I was born in Mecca. Though my mother bore seven sons, I am the only survivor. My mother passed away some years ago. I do not think she ever recovered from her broken heart at losing my elder brother," Khalil said quietly. "She often traveled with us, when we moved from place to place. She never left our side, until death called her away." His voice was soft and sad with recollection. "How about you? Where is your family?"

"My mother died when I was a baby. I don't remember her," said Laila. "My father married again two years ago." Unwittingly, resentment had crept into her voice. "My father passed away four months ago." She did not mention Naila.

"I'm sorry for your loss," said Khalil. "Life is strange, filled with many heartaches." They rode on quietly for some time, each deep in their own thoughts of stirred up memories.

"Don't you think we are prisoners of our destiny? And we must make what we can of it?" Khalil asked.

Laila shook her head forcefully, "I believe we are all free to make choices—good or bad," she said. "What would be the point if we were chained to our destiny like puppets?"

"Sometimes life feels that way," said Khalil. "Like we are stuck and cannot get out."

"Surely you believe there's a plan and purpose to everything?" Laila said. Khalil simply shrugged his shoulders.

"Maybe. I do believe there must be more than this," he said, waving his hand across the vast expanse of desert. "All this has to have a creator. If so, then there must be a reason for everything."

Laila stared up at the sky, which seemed to wrap everything up in its vast embrace. She remembered her home. Baba was gone, but she still had a sister. And her stepmom.

They rode on in silence. Shortly after sunrise the sky appeared reddish gray as clouds gathered across the horizon. Abi frowned. He judged from the formation and color of the clouds that a storm loomed ahead.

"A sand storm is imminent," Abi said. "Still, we have a few hours before those clouds are upon us. It will give us time to reach the caves before the storm becomes intense."

The camels soon wearied, as if sensing a change in the weather. It appeared that riders and animals were ready to rest. Abi searched the sky as clouds became thicker and darker. A wind picked up. Sand blew at them.

"We need to take shelter very soon," said Abi. His voice was loud and urgent.

CHAPTER 10
A SANDSTORM

"Baba, what are you reading? Can you tell me a story, Baba?" Laila asked. Baba put down the Holy Quran and turned to Laila.

"I will tell you a story from the Quran," Baba said. "A story about the people of the cave: Once a group of people sought shelter in a cave after being persecuted. They fell asleep for three hundred years. When they awoke, they were hungry. One of them was sent to buy food from the town. The townspeople were confused as the coins that were used to purchase the food were out of date—three hundred years out of date."

Upon reaching a hilly area with caves, the caravan slowed and came to a halt. Anxiety hung heavy in the air as the nervous travelers prepared for the storm. Above them, the clouds darkened as the sky turned the color of charcoal. The travelers made haste to disembark and unload the camels. Animals were tethered safely near the inside entrance of the caves. Safe inside, Laila shivered as the wind whistled through the nooks and crannies of the cave. Abi lit a fire. A gust of wind blew it out, leaving them in darkness.

"Wrap yourselves in more layers!" Abi told them. "The sand will get into your eyes, nose and ears. Wrap up well," he yelled, above the loud howling wind. Laila shuddered as the force of the storm raged on. She added on layers of clothing, feeling more like an Egyptian mummy, with slits for her eyes. Laila wondered what would have happened to them if they had remained out in the storm, with no protection against the harsh fury of wind and sand.

"We were lucky to find these caves here," said Laila.

"We have been merchants for many years. We can tell before a sand storm approaches," said Abi. "It isn't all luck."

"You have to learn to read the signs," said Khalil. "When you live in a desert, you learn to read the weather."

Abi lit another fire and they sat around it. They waited for the storm to subside. They talked of their history and of their families. Laila's mind drifted to her past, or was it the future? She wondered what would become of her. She could not imagine living in these times—away from everyone she knew—so far from her familiar world. She thought of her stepmom. She had taken such care of her father during his illness. Her stepmom had never left his side. Laila shook her head, as she regretfully remembered how resentful she had been. She had closed her mind to them, both her stepmom and her baby sister, Naila. Her shoulders sagged as a cloud of sadness engulfed her. If she could make it up, she would. Baba always said, "We must make the best of what we have." Somehow, she felt that she had let him down. With all her heart, she wished for another chance.

Laila soon drifted off into a restless sleep. She dreamed the same dream where she was running in the desert in search of the baby. She awoke to the sounds of the baby chirping cheerfully, happy to see people around her. She giggled playfully as Laila reached out to her. Laila hesitated. Would it appear strange if she held the baby? Would it give away her disguise? She decided that it didn't matter right now and reached over to hold the baby. The baby's sweet smile warmed Laila's heart. Her laughter soothed the heavy weight she carried within her.

Laila remembered her dream. Was this meant to be? *Am I here to save this baby?* Omie took her from Laila's arms and nursed her. At once contented, the baby fell gently to sleep. The day dragged on, seemingly endless.

The storm subsided to a lull, then all was quiet. The travelers managed to get some rest, though not much sleep. They ate bread and cheese, followed by a dessert of dates, which were plentiful. Omie and Zaynab had packed enough for generous servings. Dates were the one thing that grew in abundance and could replace a meal when traveling.

Once the day was over, they set out again. With little sleep, Laila was tired and found it hard to get up on the camel for another long night's journey.

As they resumed their journey, Laila's head felt groggy. She was lethargic from the restless day spent in the caves. Her eyelids drooped heavy with sleep. Her head nodded as she tried to stay awake. She was afraid she would fall off her camel if she fell asleep. She slept for some moments and awoke suddenly when her camel wobbled, and she slipped to the side of her saddle. Clinging to her camel, she climbed back onto the saddle.

"Layth, are you awake?" Khalil asked.

"Yes," mumbled Laila, half asleep.

In the still darkness, Abi's melodious voice rang out in song. Laila was wide awake now. She felt the music and sadness in his voice, and something stirred within her.

"Abi loves to sing a *Qasidah*," said Khalil.

"It's beautiful. What is he singing about?" Laila asked in a whisper, her voice was thick with emotion as she held back her tears. It was as if all her sorrows and all her pain were contained in the notes of Abi's song. It held her entranced by its beauty.

"It's a prayer and a love song; he sings of his beloved," said Khalil.

All around them lay a vast desert. With soft thudding footsteps, the camels walked in unison. The echoing a capella carried across the soft warm desert wind to their right, to their left, and all around. Everyone listened, as they journeyed onward.

The landscape changed as the caravan encountered more rocky terrain. More hills surrounded their view and the land was more rugged.

"This is dangerous terrain, as we cannot see too far in the distance. These hills are where brigands often hide and carry out surprise attacks," said Abi.

"We are prepared, Abi. Don't worry," Khalil said. "We have strength in numbers. They would be foolish to take us on."

There seemed to be a slight quickening in the movement of the camels as if they too sensed the danger without. The caravan was large in number, but was made up of mostly merchants and would not withstand a large attack of marauders. Trade routes were a temptation for robbers. Many caravans were attacked for their textiles, jewelry, perfumes, and grains. Larger caravans were in less danger, but reckless marauders were always a threat. There was a sense of foreboding as the caravan continued, each traveler hoped that their large caravan would be too big for the marauders to risk attacking.

Night passed slowly, and anxiety hung heavy over them as they cautiously traveled onward. Eventually, daylight dispelled the heavy darkness. As the sunrise lit up the sky, Abi breathed a sigh of relief.

"We are fortunate to have escaped the threat of

attack," he said. They dismounted their camels, ate their meal, and settled in for the day's rest. Laila found it hard to fall asleep. She kept hearing sounds and imagined scorpions and snakes as sleep eluded her. She caught her breath and stifled a scream when she felt something scuttle up her leg. It was a black beetle. Screaming would blow her cover for sure. Tears stung her eyes. She gritted her teeth and shoved the beetle off with the back of her hand. Still shaking, Laila ran out of her tent. She tiptoed to Omie and Zaynab's tent. As she was about to enter, Khalil appeared. He looked confused, a questioning look in his eyes told her she was putting herself at risk.

"I'm going to check on the ladies," Laila said. It was a lame excuse, she knew, but hoped it would dispel any suspicions. Khalil said nothing. Laila went inside the tent. Omie and Zaynab were still awake. The baby played happily. Laila sat with them and put aside her worries for a moment.

"You should not spend time with us. People will be suspicious," Zaynab said. "We have come too far to jeopardize our plan."

"Yes, you're right," Laila forced herself to agree. "I'm sorry." Her heart sank a little. Though she understood Zaynab's fear, she did not want to be alone right now.

Laila walked back to her tent feeling lost and alone, wondering how she would return home. She tossed and turned and eventually fell asleep. The same scene haunted her dreams.

She was running. There were sand dunes all around her as she searched frantically for something, as if her life depended on it. The wind thrashed at her. Her clothes flapped about her. Her shawl whipped around her as she fell forward, searching for something elusive. The same cry echoed in her ears.

This time, the dream continued. She kept running. She

heard the baby's cry louder as she drew nearer. She staggered into a dimly lit cave and saw the baby wrapped in a bundle. She went inside. The baby was alone with a fire lit in the distance. She picked up the baby and held her close. The covers fell back from the baby's face. It was Naila.

Laila awoke, and for some inexplicable reason she felt her heart missing the sound of her baby sister's laughter.

The sun was setting. The hustle and bustle of travelers resumed as they gathered their belongings and took down the tents. Khalil and Abi prepared to resume their journey. As they traversed the rocky terrain, they saw fires lit in the distant hills.

"I fear we will soon have unwelcome visitors. I see them in the hills," said Abi, his voice heavy, and his face lined with worry. "My relief was premature. It cannot be avoided now. If they are foolish enough to attack us, then we must fight them."

They continued onward, all the while holding on to the tenuous thread of hope. Hope that dwindled as the darkness dissipated. The light of dawn appeared as a white line over the horizon, and they were again thankful to have had another safe night's travel.

The five of them dismounted and sat together for their morning meal of yoghurt and dates.

"Are we safe now?" Laila asked.

"We can never be sure. I fear the marauders always attack when least expected," Khalil replied.

"Do not worry, we have a large caravan," said Abi. "They would be very foolish to attack us. Perhaps that is why we passed them by. Still, we must be prepared. I shall go ahead to the front tents. You two stay here with the women." Abi went ahead, holding his sword in hand.

Laila drank her last gulp of milk when the sound of thunder roared in the distance.

"Is there another storm approaching?" Laila asked. Khalil's face tightened as he jumped to his feet. His hand moved protectively over his sword. The sound grew louder as hoof-beats thundered in the distance, coming nearer and growing louder each moment.

"Marauders!" said Khalil.

CHAPTER 11
MARAUDERS ATTACK

LAILA STOOD, as if in a trance. Baba lay lifeless, wrapped in a white burial shroud. Relatives flew in from across the world. People came up to her, patted her head and offered condolences. Women sobbed aloud. In the crowded mosque, Laila felt more alone than she had ever been. Baba was gone. She was an orphan. Her grief turned to anger—anger at her stepmom and baby sister. They took away her time with Baba.

A THUNDERING SOUND RUMBLED NEARER AND LOUDER AS A group of riders appeared on horseback. Horses' hooves kicked up a storm of sand. Riders wearing black robes approached. Only their eyes were visible through their heavily covered faces. Brandishing swords as they rode, they broke up their larger group and dispersed throughout the campsite. With trepidation, Laila heard the clashing of blades ahead, together with shouting and yelling. Their sabers glinted in the sunlight.

She shuddered as she looked at Khalil. Realizing she could not sit in the safety of the tent with Zaynab, Omie, and the baby. Laila knew she had to fight with the men. Khalil grabbed a sword and handed it to her.

"I've only held a sword in fencing. Nothing as real and heavy as this!" Laila whispered, as chills shook her whole being. She pulled up the fabric wrapped around her head to cover her face. No one should see how terrified she was. Her hands shook, and her knees buckled. All she wanted was to run for her life. Yet she stood there, gritting her teeth to stop their chattering.

"Brother, be brave. Not weak like a woman!" Khalil yelled. That was all she needed to get fired up. "You look like you have never held a weapon," Khalil said, his black eyebrows were knit together in a confused frown.

Laila grabbed the sword with both hands, feeling very Mulan-like in her ineptitude. She mustered all the anger she felt. She thought of all the injustices of the world—the past and the present—and courage overcame fear.

Shouts and scuffles continued in the distance. Zaynab and Omie waited, fearful and nervous for Laila, hoping she would not be harmed and praying for her to be brave. They kept the baby as quiet as they could, all the while listening to the sounds coming from outside their tent. Two bandits wearing black turbans on their heads, brandishing curved daggers, approached them. Khalil bravely stood his ground. To Laila's horror, he taunted the ruffians.

"Cowards!" Khalil yelled, holding up his sword. "How do you dare to take the honest-earned livelihood from travelers?"

"You are merchants—that is your livelihood, and this is what we do for a living," said a short and stocky bandit as he mocked Khalil. "Do you think you children can take on our skilled swordsmanship? Get out of our way, boy. Just give us what you have in gold and jewelry." Khalil shook his head and held up his sword.

"You will have to fight me first, but you won't get far," he said as he pointed his sword at the bandit. "We outnumber you, and besides, my brother here has me covered." Khalil said as he looked over his shoulder and motioned toward Laila.

Laila shivered. Her knees knocked together, but she glared at the robbers with every bit of anger she could muster. She was thankful her face was wrapped, to hide her nervousness and chattering teeth. Only the glint in her eyes was visible.

"Get out of my way," a second bandit scowled as he pushed Khalil aside. "I don't want the blood of young boys on my hands. He looked at Laila and laughed, tugging at her shawl. Laila's face was now uncovered and burned with anger and embarrassment. More afraid being caught out on her disguise, Laila angrily wielded her sword with both hands. Her face burned, and her hands shook.

"You haven't even grown a beard yet. Your skin is as smooth as a girl's," said the robber as he threw back his head and laughed again.

The stocky bandit held up his dagger to face Khalil's sword. Laila stopped. She realized they had no chance against these marauders and was paralyzed with fear. She had to do something, for Khalil was in imminent danger. She called out to Zaynab, who was waiting, ready to hand her the rucksack that Omie had hidden in their belongings. Khalil scowled as Laila opened the small bundle. It contained a handful of coins and two amulets of gold embedded with rubies and emeralds.

"What are you doing?" Khalil asked. "This is all Omie owns." He looked ready for battle, his eyes narrowed, and his mouth set firm with determination.

"These are just rocks, they cannot compare in value to human life!" Laila said. It was a small price to pay for safe passage to Yathrib. But she felt bad giving in to the bullies.

She furiously turned to the bandits, "Is this what you want?" The man grinned and grabbed the bundle from her hands. He opened the rucksack and looked at its contents with a greedy smile. The two men laughed.

"You kids can go. We will let you live," they shouted as they turned their horses to leave.

Khalil frowned. Laila saw the quiet fury in his face.

"Don't you care that the bandits got the better of you? You handed it over to them," he said.

Laila had been terrified, but now she was angry. A minute earlier, the bandit had a dagger pointed at his throat, and now he accused her of giving in to their demands. She turned to the bandits who, now satisfied with their loot, were about to join the others to see what goods they had collected.

"You should be ashamed of yourselves!" she yelled, uncaring that their daggers still gleamed in their hands. "Your mother must be weeping for you—for sons who have turned to robbing. Shame on you, that you steal from a widow with a baby." The two bandits were startled. For a moment, one's expression softened. Then the other punched him on his arm and grabbed the goods. They pulled on their horses' reins, who kicked up their hooves, and then turned to ride off in the opposite direction, leaving a storm of dust behind them. Laila turned to Khalil.

"What good would these jewels be if you were dead— did you think of that?" Laila yelled, "I did it to save you—to save us. And you... you stand there accusing me!" She choked back a sob. She would not let her disguise slip, even though she was mad. Her face burned in mortification. Khalil stood stunned. He stared at Laila for a moment, confused at her outburst. He sighed, then abruptly turned away. Laila walked into her tent and lay down on the makeshift bed. Her heart sank. Her eyes glistened with unshed tears.

CHAPTER 12
A RAY OF HOPE

Ten-year-old Laila lay on her bed, sobbing. She felt her heart would break from sorrow. Baba was there to comfort her. He was there to make her see. Just as morning comes after night, there is light at the end of a tunnel.

"Even in your darkest moments, you must hold on to hope with all your heart—for that is when you need it most. And I promise you, my Beti, that is when you are closest to God, so turn to the Almighty." Baba said it softly as he wiped away her tears.

A FULL MOON SPILLED SILVER LIGHT ONTO THE SANDS, which shimmered like water dazzled by sunlight. The excitement had settled down. Abi had returned to inform Khalil and Laila that they had fought off the marauders. A few trinkets here and there were taken, but for the most part everything was intact. There were a few bruises, a few hurt egos, but no serious loss.

The caravan prepared for its journey on the fourth evening. Everything shone luminous and dreamlike. Laila gasped as she took in the view, so different in the evening from the molten gold of daytime. They were lucky to escape unharmed from their encounter with the marauders, minus a few jewels.

The camels were loaded, and Zaynab, Omie, and the baby sat silently in the *Shuqduf*. One day remained before they arrived in the city of Yathrib, where the Messenger of God was transforming lives with his new teachings of one God, of justice and equality for all. Omie watched Laila's head sunken low, her shoulders drooping. She sensed Laila's disappointment in having given away their valuables. She called to her. About to mount her camel, Laila went to see Omie. She reached out and took Laila by the hand.

"I did not know this day would come," Omie said. "I only hoped that my baby would live to see the Messenger of God. I only hoped she would have a chance of growing up in a better world—and now, thanks to you, we have that chance. What good are jewels? They are mere stones when we are not free."

"Thank you. I'm sorry you had to give up all your valuables," said Laila with a forced smile, though her eyes were clouded deep with sadness.

"Do not worry, my child, the Merciful One will provide for us if we put our trust in His Wisdom. He is the One, the Guide, the Life-Giver. I put my complete trust in Him before, and you came to help us from another land, another place far from here." Laila nodded as tears welled up in her eyes. Omie truly believed in her. Laila felt she did not deserve such trust.

"And besides that, my child," Omie whispered, as she pulled out the medallion hanging discreetly around her neck. "I still have this. This is my most valuable jewelry."

Laila stared at its familiar image. Perhaps she had seen it somewhere in a museum. "This was given to me by my mother, and to my mother by hers. It has been in my family since ancient times. They say we are descendants of Abraham, so who knows how long this has been in my family?" Laila smiled, and her tears dried. The medallion glimmered in the moonlight. It hung clumsily around Omie's delicate neck. Bold gold beads hung in a chain with a chunky, disk-shaped pendant carved with intricate leafy designs. Omie slipped the medallion back into its safe hiding place beneath her layers of clothing. The important thing was that they were safe, ready for their night journey again, after the day's misadventure. Laila smiled shakily and walked over to her camel. She rubbed Jemel's neck gently as he wobbled to standing position. Holding on tight, Laila breathed a sigh as the caravan slowly moved forward. The camels plodded along patiently in the darkening night.

Silently, the camels made their way through the vast expanse of desert. They passed by hills and barren *wadis,* thirstily awaiting the rains when they would be filled again as reservoirs to quench the thirst of wandering travelers. The desert was a cruel and lonely place, Laila thought, yet there was a beauty in it that surprised her.

Khalil did not speak. He was deep in thought. Laila wondered where this would end, and how she would return home. Home. Chicago seemed a world away!

The cool night air carried a welcoming breeze after the fiery heat of the day. Laila felt that time was slipping away. Feeling a sense of urgency, she called out to Khalil.

"Where will you go after you leave us in Yathrib?" she said.

"We will be traveling to Syria and further on to Persia. Why do you ask?" Khalil said.

"You must have seen many different people, many different lands. What was it like?" Laila asked. Khalil looked directly at Laila; his eyes were dark and set deep in a face the color of burnished sand.

"In all my travels, I have not met anyone as stubborn as you! You let those robbers get the better of you," he said. "Why did you not let me take them out?"

"You don't have to settle everything with swords and daggers. Sometimes you can get people to change their minds. Maybe not this time, but sometimes," said Laila. She searched Khalil's mystified expression.

"So you feel sorry for these brigands and say: There's no need to rob us, here you may take all our things..." he said sarcastically.

"Maybe the robbers will think twice before they rob again. I mean, there are ways to come to a solution. Perhaps they don't have any option but to rob. Maybe that's all they know. What if they have options to make an honest living... options to live a more peaceful life?" Laila said, ignoring the sting of Khalil's comments. "At least we can try to communicate with them."

"It's difficult to communicate when someone's pointing a sword in your face," said Khalil, and sighed with exasperation. It seemed they were not going to agree. Laila confused him. He didn't understand her way of thinking. "They say the Messenger of God talks of peace and a new way of life," he said quietly changing the topic.

"Yes. That is why we are going to Yathrib," Laila replied. "There is a chance for the baby to live and to lead a better life."

Khalil was thoughtful. "I have spent all my years traveling with merchants from place to place. I meet many people in different lands I have seen, but almost everywhere I go I see greed in some form or another. We get good prices for products we trade, and we consider our deal successful. These ideas you talk about are different. They do not bring riches or trade. Why do you do it?" He looked at Laila, his bright eyes questioning.

"Why not?" she said and shrugged her shoulders. "What use is our life if we don't help each other? My father always said, 'The most certain thing in life is that we will die, and when we die the only thing that will matter is how we lived...'"

Khalil was quiet for a moment before speaking. "Yes, that is true, our lives are like a container of sand, softly spilling through to the other side. I will speak to Abi. Maybe he will want to see this Messenger everyone speaks of."

Laila was surprised. "You would do that? You would change your plans?" she asked, "for us?" She caught her breath in surprise.

"Anything for my brother," Khalil said. A smile spread across his face, as he turned his camel and moved forward to catch up with his father.

"Or sister," whispered Laila. She felt deceitful but what other way was there to save the baby?

Stars burned bright in the dark velvet sky and warmth filled her heart.

Daylight crept into the vast desert sky. Purplish pinks chased away the darkness of night, followed by the orange of burnished gold. As the colors rose, so the temperatures soared. The baby was restless. Everyone felt the stifling heat. Laila's clothing was sticky with sweat. She could use a long, cool shower. Though she was glad the journey was near its end, she felt a fear in the pit of her stomach. Fear gripped her, as she wondered about the uncertain future. She wondered if she had a future. She shook her head, as if to shake away the anxiety. She hoped Khalil would convince his father to change his plans of going on to Syria. Instead, she hoped he would go with them to Yathrib. She waited with baited breath, watching father and son riding ahead of her in deep discussion.

They settled into their makeshift campsite once

again. The heat was excruciating, more so today, Laila felt. As they sat down to eat, Abi was quiet, as if thinking deeply about some matter.

"Khalil has convinced me to change my plan," Abi said looking at Laila and Zaynab, then at Omie and the baby. "I have been waiting for Khalil to take some initiative in decision making. I am getting old and have waited for this day—when my son will become a man," Abi said with a smile.

Laila was grateful Abi had listened to Khalil. Abi agreed with Khalil that it would be far safer to escort them all the way to Yathrib. It may not be a wise business decision, but it was a humane and compassionate one, Abi decided. Leaving them unescorted would mean disaster.

"I heard many stories of the Messenger of God in places I visited with my trade," said Abi. "I heard stories of his honesty when he was a tradesman, many years ago, when I was much younger myself. I will visit the city of the Messenger and bring some trade to Yathrib as a peace offering."

"May God reward you brother," said Omie. "We are indebted to you for your kindness in taking us aboard, but we never expected you to escort us all the way, jeopardizing your caravan." Omie's eyes shone with unshed tears, as she hugged her baby closer to her.

"I have never done anything without looking for some profit. I think the time has come to slow down, and do something worthy that will not fill my bag with gold, but perhaps help my soul," Abi said.

Laila had no idea how they would have managed to get to Yathrib on their own. All she knew was she had made a promise to help a baby, and she trusted that whatever got them that far would get them to their destination. She felt something guiding them. It was not something she could explain. She could just feel it, and she trusted it would take her home. Was that faith, she wondered? It felt like she knew in her heart that things would work out, it took away her fear, leaving behind hope in its place.

Abi discussed his plans with the group of travelers at the head of the caravan. They would part ways at the next oasis. Their point of departure was decided upon. Abi would lead their group with twenty camels toward Yathrib, while the remaining caravan of over one hundred camels would continue onward north, toward Syria as planned. Their smaller group was vulnerable, but Abi did not seem perturbed, as it was only a few more hours to Yathrib. To their destination.

"What will you do when you get to Yathrib?" Khalil asked.

Laila was silent. She did not know how to answer him, or how to explain.

"I don't know," she said, shrugging her shoulders. This was the last day before their journey's end. Laila busied herself with feeding Jemel. He had carried her across the desert safely. She patted his head as he munched on the dry desert brush that grew in abundance around them.

"I will miss you, dear friend," she whispered as the camel looked at her with his large eyes that were hooded by thick lashes. He nudged her with his head, as if in reply.

"We will be there tomorrow, God-willing," said Omie, watching Laila with the camel. "You have been a great blessing to us."

Laila's face flushed, she clasped her arms about her, not knowing what to say.

"Your eyes are black as night, like your name, Laila. I will not forget you," said Omie.

She took a pouch from the folds of her robe. "Here, Laila. This is for you." Omie handed the pouch to Laila. Laila accepted the pouch, which was fabric rolled into a small package and tied with thread. She untied the thread and unrolled the fabric. Inside was a lock of the baby's hair. She wrapped it up again and put it in her pocket beneath the layers of her clothing.

"Thank you," she whispered, her voice thick with emotion.

"I have named my baby Laila after you," said Omie. Laila blushed, thinking she did not deserve the honor. She nervously looked around to see if anyone had heard. Khalil was with Abi setting up the tents. Laila figured she should be helping the men, but she stayed with Zaynab and the newly named baby, Laila.

The travelers were soon done eating, and everyone settled in for their last day of rest. Tomorrow they would be in Yathrib. The sun was high in the sky, and Laila parted from Zaynab and Omie to go to her tent. As she lay on her bed, she went over the events of the last few days. It had been an incredible and dangerous adventure. If she ever got to share it with Beth, she doubted even *she* would believe her.

Lying on the makeshift bed, Laila felt her lungs constrict. She pulled out her inhaler and took a puff. Aftertaking a long deep breath, she felt the tightness in her lungs ease a little. She took a second puff and felt her lungs relax and unwind what felt like a tight knot in her lungs. Sometimes yoga helped, she thought, and sat up cross-legged and closed her eyes. She calmed her breathing. Her doctor said her asthma attacks were often psychosomatic—very often induced by emotional stress. She took deep breaths, with both her eyes closed. She focused on staying calm and centered. She was deep into her breathing exercises when she heard Khalil's voice.

"Is that a new worship ritual?" Khalil asked. He stood at the entrance to her tent. *So much for privacy!* Laila thought.

"No, I do this to help calm my breathing. It helps me,"

Laila said, slipping her inhaler back in her pocket, hoping Khalil did not see. It would not do to have a twenty-first century item left behind in the seventh century. Khalil stared at Laila in surprise. Laila suddenly realized she wasn't wearing her turban. She looked around and grabbed the turban. Her eyes met Khalil's. She saw shock register on his face, then disbelief followed by anger. Her disguise was up.

"You won't tell," she whispered hoarsely. Khalil shook his head from side to side. Shock was followed by deathly silence. He stared at Laila.

"You're a girl," he said with quiet anger.

CHAPTER 13
END OF THE JOURNEY

"God does not look at your bodies nor your forms, but at your hearts and your actions."

"You know why I did it?" Laila whispered.

"Why? Why the need for deception?" he asked, his face twitched as he turned and kicked a stone. "If Abi finds out he will be furious—and may even change our route or even throw you out. Why would you do this?" Laila drew in her breath sharply, startled at the anger in his voice.

"For the baby and Omie," she whispered, and wished she would disappear into the sand as her heart sank further into the pit of her stomach. Laila wished she had never arrived there in the first place. Laila watched as Khalil stood quietly. His forehead creased into a frown, as though deep in thought. As if remembering every conversation that they had together.

"Why can't we continue for one more day, just the same? For Omie and her baby?" Laila pleaded.

"It's different now; we can't be the same when everything has changed," said Khalil. He sighed and spun around to walk away.

"Why does it have to be different?" Laila said. Khalil stopped in his tracks and turned. "Why can't you speak to me as you did before, without seeing the outer self? Why can't you see me as an equal soul, a human being just like you?"

"You take a great risk. It is a big sacrifice to make for someone," Khalil said quietly.

"Where I come from, a disguise would not be necessary. Men and women are equal," Laila said, suddenly feeling angry at the injustice of it all. "Girls are treated fairly, or at least the laws require that they are."

"I knew you were different," said Khalil, with a deep sigh. "It now makes sense."

"Does it change everything?" Laila asked.

"You are who you are—if not a brother, then a sister." Khalil's expression appeared torn, as if he were trying to convince himself. "We have faced a treacherous journey together—I can handle this." His face was serious. No brotherly smile was offered as he stared long and hard at Laila, as if he were about to say more. Suddenly, he turned and walked back to his tent. Laila's face burned. Her hands felt clammy and a ball of anger twisted into knots in her stomach. Tears hovered behind her lashes, but she blinked them away, shaking her head. She wrapped her arms around herself, her head hung low. She felt more alone than she had ever been. She lay down on her mat and let the tears flow. She fell into an exhausted sleep. She dreamed the same dream. She was running and running in the midst of a sand storm. She was lost.

Laila awoke as the sun was about to set. As darkness fell, the moon's silver light spilled over the black hills that hovered in the distance. They were close to Medina, as the city of Yathrib would come to be named. It was well known for its black hills. It was just a few hours' camel ride away. Laila wondered if it could be possible that she would meet the Messenger of God in person. She could hardly imagine meeting the revered Prophet beloved by more than a billion people in her time and throughout history. Ballads and Hymns have been sung in praise of him for centuries. It seemed impossible to believe that there was a chance that she could meet him. Omie, Zaynab and the baby would be safe, so her job was done, if this is what she came to do.

They rested for part of the night and then began the last leg of their journey. The caravan continued in the middle of the night, only a few hours away from Yathrib.

"We are heading out later, as we want to arrive during the daytime," said Abi. "We do not wish to surprise them in the middle of the night, by arriving stealthily like robbers."

They rode in silence for much of the way. The distant black hills grew nearer and loomed larger before them.

Crowds gathered at the city entrance as sentinels, guarding their precious inhabitant: the Messenger of God. The people of Yathrib were known for their open hearts. They had joyfully welcomed the Messenger and his followers into their city. As the caravan of camels drew near, a group of people gathered around. Their faces were grim and suspicious as they faced the weary travelers.

"We come in peace," Abi said, as he raised his hand to his heart.

"No trade arrives from Mecca," a young man yelled. "The Meccans have sent spies!"

His shouts drew an even larger crowd of young boys, men, and elders of the community, each one willing to defend their beloved Messenger from harm. Laila shuddered. They had traveled this far, through all these days and nights. Had they faced so much hardship, only to be turned away at the last moment? Her heart missed a beat as she waited to hear the outcome.

"We come in peace with an offering to our Messenger," Abi said as he and Khalil dismounted their camels and walked forward to reassure the people of the city. They stood in deep conversation with a group of village elders.

In the distance, a melodious voice echoed a call to prayer, "God is great! God is great! God is great! God is great! I testify that there is no deity but God! I testify there is no deity but God! I testify that Muhammad is His messenger! I testify that Muhammad is His messenger! Come to prayer! Come to prayer! Come to success! Come to success! God is great! God is great!"

La-illaha-illa-llah! The familiar words of the *Adhan* reminded Laila of the times she went for prayers at the mosque with Baba. The leader of the group spoke some more with Khalil's father. After some discourse between the people, it was decided that the visitors were trustworthy, and welcome to enter Yathrib.

"Come and join us for prayer and meet the Messenger of God!" An elderly man said to Khalil and Abi. Laila and Zaynab dismounted. Crowds of people watched them as they walked their camels into the city. Khalil, Zaynab, and Laila each held onto the reins of a camel, steadily guiding them. Omie sat in the *Shuqduf* with the baby. The camels seemed to sense that after a long journey, they were finally home.

The crowd stopped before the small building that was the mosque. Laila felt a tingling sensation as she prepared to meet the Messenger of God. Suddenly, she felt afraid and excited at the same time. Butterflies fluttered in her stomach. The midday sun's glare was bright in her eyes. A sudden gust of wind whipped at her turban. She held onto it, shivering a little. The wind whipped at her and surrounded her in a haze of dust, misting her view. She saw the shadow of someone approaching from a distance. She looked at Khalil, who seemed to become dimmer, as the dust thickened about her and clouded her view. It whirled around her, twisting and spinning like a tornado. She was in the center of a storm, feeling lost, dizzy, and helpless. The last thing she heard was the gurgling laugh of the baby, safe in her mother's arms.

CHAPTER 14
BACK TO THE PRESENT

"Laila, my Beti," Baba said. His voice was serious. "Sometimes life deals you blows. And that is when you must hold on hard to your faith. That is when you have to be brave and strong."

"What is it, Baba?" Laila asked, her heart pounding fearfully, as she sensed his sadness.

"It's cancer," said Baba quietly. And the walls of her tender faith began to crumble.

Laila awoke to the buzzing and beeping machines. She moved her head as her eyes adjusted to her surroundings. She was hooked up to machines in a hospital bed. Her head throbbed. Her left arm was sore. She dragged her right arm over the sheet and felt an IV tube taped on her left arm. An oximeter blinked on her finger. She gasped, panic arising as she tried to sit up in the hospital bed. *The baby! Was the baby safe?* She wondered as she flopped back down, too tired to sit.

"What's happening... are they safe? I need to know if the baby's safe!" she croaked, and struggled to sit up again, then fell back on her pillow.

"Laila, dear," her aunt said, wiping tears from her eyes. "You're back with us. It's okay. You're fine now, thank God."

"Laila," said Uncle Farid, his eyes red from lack of sleep. "You've been gone for twenty-four hours..." Laila looked at her aunt and uncle.

"Please," she whispered, "tell me... what happened? Why am I here?" Her aunt and uncle exchanged looks, then Uncle Farid spoke.

"Look, we don't know how, but you passed out during *Tawaf*. In fact, you were standing by the Black Stone as if in a trance. The crowd moved away from you. It was the strangest thing," said Uncle Farid. He shook his head as if to shake off the memory. "I've never seen anything like it. You were standing there, yet it was like you weren't there... It was as if your body was there, but not you." His voice shook with emotion.

"The doctors have been mystified," said Aunt Balqees. "They couldn't find anything wrong. First, they thought you must have had sunstroke, but they ruled that out as there was no fever, and all the tests were normal."

Uncle Farid shook his head, "Nothing was wrong with you... You were simply unconscious. All your vitals are good."

"It was like you were sleeping," said Aunt Balqees. She patted Laila's arm gently, as if to make sure she was all right. "Perhaps it was the heat, who knows?"

The clouds in her mind began to disperse, and Laila remembered. She remembered her five-day trek through the desert. How would she explain her journey to anyone? How could anyone believe her? She didn't know if it was real or just a dream. She hardly believed it herself.

"We had to tell Raisa," said Uncle Farid. "She kept calling. When there was no change in your condition, we couldn't keep it from her."

Laila sat up, feeling a burst of energy. "I have to call Beth, I promised I would video chat every day."

"All in good time," Uncle Farid said. "We're planning to fly back to Chicago as soon as you're well enough to travel."

"They should discharge you today, now that you're back with us," said Aunt Balqees. "We can get you checked out again as soon as we return to Chicago." But Laila was not listening. All her thoughts were with the baby and her companions fourteen hundred years away in time. "They're dead," she whispered, "and I don't even know if they were okay." Tears ran down her cheeks as she stared up at the ceiling.

CHAPTER 15
HOME IN CHICAGO

Seven-year-old Laila sat with her father, planting tulip bulbs in the back yard.

"Can we stay like this forever, Baba? It's such a perfect day. I want to keep this day as it is forever," said Laila, as she placed a small bulb in the hole she made in the ground and covered it softly with dirt.

"Ah my Beti, if only... but where there's time, there is a start and a finish. There's no room for forever. Everything has its time," said Baba, "and for everything, time runs out."

"Why can't we stop time? Then it will be forever!" said Laila.

"Time is like sand. If you hold sand in your hands, it runs through your fingers. Time slips away. Just like sand," said Baba.

Laila looked out the window for the twentieth time and thought of Omie, Zaynab, Khalil, and her namesake, baby Laila. Her stomach reeled when she thought of them, wondering if the baby survived. How would she ever know? Laila wondered as an anxiety gripped her. Did she grow up? Did she have a good life? And what of Zaynab and Khalil— thoughts of them invaded her mind and her sleep. She wondered if she should tell Beth. Would anyone believe her? Would they think she was losing her mind? Perhaps she was. She could not help wondering and worrying about the baby.

A car's engine whirred outside. Laila looked out the window and saw Beth's mom give her a hug and drive off. She skipped down the stairs and opened the door just as Beth was about to ring the doorbell. Beth entered and both friends hugged each other.

"So how was it? Beth asked, looking at Laila. "You look different."

The living room was filled with boxes of all sizes. Both girls moved away from the front door. Laila's stepmom was packing the kitchen things into a box. She stood up, wiped a hand over her forehead and waved to Beth.

"Hey, Beth, good to see you," she said.

"Hi, Mrs. Saleem. How's Naila doing?"

"She's still got that lingering cold, so I put her down for a nap."

Naila had been sleeping a lot since Laila's return, so Laila had not had time to play with her sister.

"So, tell me all about it," said Beth, turning to Laila. "I can see that you're dying share something."

"Look Beth—you've known me practically all my life," said Laila turning around and skipping up the stairs to her bedroom. Beth followed her into the room where a suitcase stood in the middle of the rug.

"Yeah, since Kindergarten," said Beth. "I guess that's the same as knowing you all your life."

"If I told you something really fantastic—like out of this world crazy—would you believe me?" asked Laila, hesitating a little as she clasped and unclasped her hands.

"Try me," said Beth. "I'm all ears." She flung herself on the bed with her arms folded behind her head, waiting to hear Laila's story.

As Laila related the whole sequence of events that transpired, from the moment she left Chicago to the moment she came to in the hospital, it seemed fantastical to be real, even to her own ears.

"Sounds crazy, doesn't it?" said Laila, waiting for Beth's reaction.

"Sure does," said Beth.

"You believe me, don't you?" asked Laila, feeling if Beth didn't believe her story, then she must be going out of her mind. Beth nodded.

"If you say this happened to you, then I believe you," said Beth. Laila breathed a sigh of relief, but her eyes clouded over as she thought of the baby.

"I just wish I could know that she was fine," Laila said. Then she shook her head, and remembered her gift for Beth. "Here, I have a souvenir for you. I got it at the airport, as there wasn't any time... to go shopping really."

"Yep, it must have been pretty difficult, seeing as you were unconscious in the hospital," Beth said with a laugh. Laila pulled her suitcase, laid it flat and opened it. She rummaged through her clothes in search of something. She pulled out her *abaya*. As she unwrapped it, Beth beheld a silver lamp, very much like Aladdin's lamp. "There!" Laila said with a flourish as she handed it to Beth. "I thought you'd like this. I wanted to keep it safe, so I wrapped it in my clothes for extra protection. It's pretty fragile."

"It's really cool," said Beth. "Thank you." Beth got down on the rug and held the lamp in both hands, looking at the intricate details carved into it. "This is really beautiful, I feel afraid to rub it, in case a genie appears."

The two girls laughed.

Laila was still holding the *abaya*. Then she felt the lump in its pocket, and suddenly remembered Omie's gift. She slipped her hand into the pocket and pulled out the folded fabric. She gasped as goosebumps curled the hairs on her neck. A chill ran down her spine. It couldn't be.

"What's wrong Laila? You look awfully pale, all of a sudden," said Beth. Laila didn't reply. She held out the fabric to Beth.

"It's still here," whispered Laila. "The baby's hair, it was in my pocket."

"Is that what Zaynab's mom gave you? The baby's lock of hair?" Laila nodded. "Now you've got proof," Beth said, getting excited.

Laila held the folded fabric gently, remembering those long gone who once walked this earth. "You can give it in for the DNA test we're doing next week." Beth said.

"I couldn't really. I mean, Mrs. Mullings said it has to be hair with roots at the end," Laila said, looking at the soft lock of hair in her hand. She didn't want to part with this token. It was a special memory.

"But it would be awesome to see what we could find out," Beth said.

"What if I could find out if the baby survived? It would be worth it then," said Laila.

"I say do it, Laila," said Beth. "The chances are, they will find out where it came from. That will give us proof of your story—not that we need proof, but wouldn't it be awesome?"

"Yeah kind of," said Laila, getting excited about the DNA test now. "Let's do it!"

CHAPTER 16

THE FIELD TRIP

FIVE-YEAR-OLD LAILA SAT *in the car seat. She pulled on her seat belt; it clicked in place.*

"Baba, why do bad things happen?" she asked.

"Don't worry, Beti Laila, nothing bad will happen to you while your Baba is here," said Baba.

"But why did Beth break her arm? That's bad," said Laila.

"We can't control everything that happens, and there are some bad things that happen," said Baba. "I don't have all the answers, I just know that things work out in the end."

"But why, Baba, why?" asked Laila.

"Sometimes you just need faith," Baba said. "You ask a lot of questions, Laila, Beti."

"Isn't that how I will learn?" asked Laila. Baba nodded.

"Yes, my Beti, yes indeed it is," he smiled at her upturned face, full of curiosity for her world.

"What is faith, Baba?" Laila asked.

"Faith is love," said Baba.

. . .

THE DAY OF THE SCHOOL FIELD TRIP ARRIVED. LAILA checked her bag for the tenth time to see that she had the baby's lock of hair. It was there, placed safely in a zip lock bag. She made sure nothing had touched it, so it was exactly as it was when Omie handed it to her. She was nervous and feeling torn. Was she being dishonest? She questioned herself and had second thoughts many times. Whenever she had doubts, Beth encouraged her. Emboldened by her friend's enthusiasm, Laila was determined to go through with it.

The class spilled out of the bus on to the stone steps of the museum. They made their way up the stairs, past the grand stone pillars and through the green revolving doors. The two large elephants were there as always, and at the end of the hall stood a huge dinosaur skeleton. Laila noticed a pterodactyl suspended from wires, as if in flight. She hadn't noticed that before. Her nervousness seemed to heighten her senses.

"We will be going up the south staircase," Mrs. Mullings told the students as they lined up into the museum lobby.

"Notice that arched space about the staircase. It's an apse," continued Mrs. Mullings as they followed her up the stairs. Laila's hand felt clammy as she walked up the stairs, trailing her hand nervously on the wrought iron balustrade.

"We will turn to your right, where you see the Gems Exhibit, then follow the signs past the meteorites and toward the DNA Discovery Center," Mrs. Mullings said. Laila followed the line of students as they passed gems of all shapes and sizes, followed by the geological section.

Laila stopped to look at a large meteorite. What thousand-year-old secrets did it hold? Laila wondered. She hadn't realized she was standing with her head to the glass, thinking back to another time, and another stone. She shook her head, turned and followed the group to the DNA Discovery Center.   They looked through the window, and watched as the scientists sat at work, on view for all passersby. A young woman looked up from her computer and waved at them. She motioned to her right and disappeared. Moments later she appeared from the side door and greeted them.

"Everyone, I'd like you to meet Dr. Waldron, the scientist who will be working with us. She's also my baby sister," said Mrs. Mullings with some pride in her bubbly voice. "Take it away sis," she added with a smile.

"Good morning students," Dr. Waldron said. "I'm really excited that you're here today. We have an amazing new test that you will get to take part in. But first things first. Let's begin with a tour of our lab, where great research is being done."

"They don't look like sisters," Beth whispered to Laila, who nodded. Mrs. Mullings was bubbly with an effervescence that spilled over and was contagious. Her sister was calm and, though not serious, you could hardly call her cheerful. They all followed Dr. Waldron and Mrs. Mullings into the side door that took them into the lab. It seemed smaller than Laila imagined. She noticed a picture of Phil Collins on the wall.

"They've got good taste in music," Laila whispered to Beth, who giggled when she saw what Laila pointed out. She knew him because Baba had often played music by Genesis.

"Here we have a huge DNA Sequencer—or analyzer machine—that cost three billion dollars just ten years ago," said Dr. Waldron. "In ten years, the same sequencing was done with this smaller machine, at a much smaller cost of $1000 dollars. What I'm trying to explain is that scientific research is progressing so fast that we are making amazing and fantastic discoveries each day."

They followed their teacher and Dr. Waldron around

the lab, meeting the scientists as they took a tour of their laboratory.

"Now comes the exciting part," said Dr. Waldron. "Now we have a smaller machine that not only gives you your DNA history, but it also carbon dates every sample. We can figure out so much more with this new discovery."

"But first things first. Today you will get to give your DNA samples to discover your history. I will talk a little about mitochondrial DNA matches and how we break down the cells to release the DNA. If you have any questions, just raise your hand."

"You all get to ask a question each from the list you've prepared; otherwise we may be here until evening," Mrs. Mullings added.

"After we collect your samples, we then identify and isolate only those regions of DNA that are informative genetic markers. It all may sound confusing right now, but we will explain it further," said Dr. Waldron.

"Yes?" Dr. Waldron looked at Cole who had raised his hand.

"So, what exactly is DNA?" asked Cole.

Mrs. Mullings looked at Cole.

"We have covered this in class ..." she said.

"That's totally fine. All questions are welcome. DNA is a tiny molecule that provides the instructions for how an organism grows, develops, and functions."

"What are you working on?" asked Greg.

"Thank you, we are working on sharks, lichens, and birds right now," said Dr. Waldron. "Before I continue, I just want to say there's no such thing as a bad question. We can only learn from asking questions, and it takes courage to ask questions, so thank you for your question, young man. With today's research we can pinpoint exactly where your ancestors came from. It's like a trail of history, so it's worth it. We can find out so much from just a tiny sample. Every day we are learning more from this."

"What is the coolest thing you've worked on?" Gia asked.

"I've done diagnostic tests on birds, to determine if they are infected with malarial pathogens called haemosporidians." said Dr. Waldron.

"Cool," said Beth.

"Sounds like a monster from Doctor Who," said Laila. "Haemosporidians."

Mrs. Mullings sat with the students, enthralled, as Dr. Waldron put on gloves and walked through the whole process step-by-step on how to discover DNA.

"I want to share a recent break-through," said Dr. Waldron, "We have already developed ways to isolate markers for sequencing and determining individual haplo-groups," she explained. "But now we can actually tell exactly where and when each of your ancestors were in specific parts of the world. You could say we have a way of touching our past. We can read more information from the DNA tests than ever before."

Everyone listened as Dr. Waldron carefully and painstakingly collected samples from each student, patiently answering questions and repeatedly going through each sample's process to determine the results of their ancestry.

Laila felt hot and cold. She shifted and fidgeted in her chair. Her breakfast jumped somersaults in her stomach.

"It will take a week before the results are out," said Dr. Waldron. "I would be happy to deliver the results to your school in person."

Mrs. Mullings beamed with delight.

"Thank you!" she said. "You have no idea the favor Dr. Waldron is bestowing upon our school. This is a fantastic new breakthrough in science and you get to be part of it."

The excitement in their teacher's voice increased the

level of excitement in the students, and there was a hum of voices ringing in the room. The teachers had given them the option to choose whether to give a hair sample or saliva. As it turned out, they were both equally accurate at producing results.

Laila carefully took out the sample that she had carried with her. The technician came around to collect each sample in its own individual sterile container. Students were given gloves to handle everything, so as not to contaminate their sample.

"Is that your hair young lady?" asked the technician when Laila handed over the hair sample in a clear container. She held her breath, waiting to be caught out. Her face went pale as she looked at the technician eyeing her sample. Before she could open her mouth to speak, he laughed, "Just checking to make sure. Don't look so serious." He proceeded to move on collecting from the rest of the students. Laila breathed again.

It was done. There was no going back. She sighed with relief. Beth nudged her.

"Are you okay?" Beth asked.

"I guess," said Laila.

"So, you did it then?" asked Beth. Laila nodded. "Now we have to wait. I'm so excited."

Laila's pulse raced. She was nervous and fearful of what the results would prove.

CHAPTER 17
THE PRINCIPAL'S OFFICE

Eighteen Months Earlier:
Laila sat with Baba in the principal's office.

"Mr. Saleem, it's good to see you. So, what brings you and Laila to my office today?" asked Mrs. Deere.

"We would like to request some time off for Laila.... you see, Laila and I are going on a pilgrimage to Mecca," said Baba.

Mrs. Deere was thoughtful.

"Laila is a very good student, but this is an important year for her. Would it be possible to go during the school vacation?" Mrs. Deere asked.

"I understand your concerns very well. I am against Laila missing school, but this is an opportunity I don't wish her to miss," Baba said. "The pilgrimage, or Hajj, occurs only once a year, so I cannot choose the dates. It is a very significant spiritual journey, to be undertaken once in a lifetime. I feel Laila is at an age where she will appreciate this journey."

"Mr. Saleem, because Laila is such a good student, I am willing to make an exception. There has never been a single complaint from any teacher—they have only ever praised her. You must be very proud *of your daughter," said Mrs. Deere, "but we will need a formal request in writing."*

"Of course, I will get a letter to you as soon as possible," said Baba, "And thank you. I really appreciate your help."

LAILA SAT IN HER BEDROOM, SURROUNDED BY BOXES. They were moving soon, so she packed her books into boxes. She remembered packing just a few weeks earlier for Mecca. She felt the same gnawing in her stomach as she wondered what became of the baby—and Zaynab, Khalil and Omie. She shook her head and hoped the DNA test would reveal something. She had just finished packing a row of books from the top bookshelf, when the phone rang. Laila heard her stepmother take the call into the kitchen.

"Hello," Laila heard her stepmom's voice as she answered the phone; then her voice became low and muffled. Laila's ears perked up when she overheard her name mentioned. She was curious. Her stepmom raised her voice. Her tone sounded like she was arguing with someone. Laila felt she should not be eavesdropping, but they were discussing her, and the serious tone of her stepmom's voice gave her a strange feeling in the pit of her stomach, a feeling that something was not right.

"I am sure it's all just a simple misunderstanding," said her stepmom to the caller.

Her stepmom put down the phone abruptly and came looking for Laila.

"Is everything okay?" asked Laila.

"We have a meeting with the principal tomorrow morning," she said, looking unusually flustered.

"Was that the school? What did they want?" asked Laila.

"It was the principal. She made a very serious claim....

I can't believe she could accuse you of stealing," her step-mom's voice shook, brimming with anger. Laila had never seen her like that. She hadn't asked Laila if she had done anything. She trusted her. Laila felt alarmed. She hoped everything would be all right. Why would they accuse her of stealing? Whatever could they mean?

"I'll call the baby sitter. We can't take Naila, she's still feeling under the weather," her stepmom said.

Beth came over later that day.

"What do you think the principal means?" asked Beth, after Laila told her about the morning phone call. "I mean accusing you of stealing—that's really big. She wouldn't do that lightly, or without evidence."

"What evidence do you think she would have?" asked Laila, "I didn't take anything."

"Do you think it's related to the DNA testing?" asked Beth.

"I'm not sure—it has to be, but why and how? I can't figure out what it could be," said Laila exhaling sharply. "I'm so confused."

Laila tried not to worry about the phone call. She would find out soon enough when she met with the principal the next day. She was surprised how her stepmom had stood up for her. She was surprised how angry her stepmom was that the principal could suspect her of such a thing as steal-ing. *She has a higher opinion of me than I thought—or expected.* She had been trying to spend more time with her stepmom and Naila since she returned from Mecca. With their immi-nent move to an apartment, and school and homework, there was a lot going on right now.

The next day, Laila and her stepmom went to school together. They went straight to the office where the secre-tary asked them to wait a minute while she told the principal they were there.

Laila clenched her fists in her pockets. She felt her shoulders tense. She wondered what it could be that brought such a serious accusation. *What if she were suspended?* Butterflies fluttered in her stomach. She felt nauseous and wanted it all to be over.

"The principal will see you in her office," said the secretary. Laila and her stepmom both stood up together. Laila saw her stepmom's face was strained. *She's worried too.* Laila appreciated the support. They followed the secretary into the principal's office.

"Good morning," said Mrs. Deere. "I appreciate you coming this morning. Please have a seat." Laila sat down in the chair next to her stepmom, facing Mrs. Deere's stern look. This was the first time Laila was in the principal's office since Baba brought her a couple of years ago. That was a different reason; in fact, it was as different as it could possibly be.

CHAPTER 18
THE ACCUSATION

Seventeen months earlier....

"Laila, Beti, I have something to tell you."

"Baba, have you booked the tickets? When are we going for Hajj?"

Baba took Laila's hand and held it in his. Laila looked up at him.

"Sometimes we make plans, but they don't work out. I'm sorry Beti, we won't be going on Hajj this year."

"But why?" Laila shook her shoulders, and pursed her lips petulantly, "Is it because of her?"

"Try to call her Ammi. It isn't so difficult," Baba said softly. Laila knew it was. How could she call her stepmom Ammi—mother?

"Why aren't we going?" asked Laila again, as her brows knitted together in a frown.

"Raisa is expecting a baby, and she is not doing very well. It wouldn't be right to leave her at this time," Baba said. "We will have another opportunity, if God wills."

"Please have a seat," said Mrs. Deere, looking

uncomfortable. "I know this isn't easy for you. It was such a shock for me—for all the staff."

"What exactly are you accusing *my daughter* of?" asked Laila's stepmom. Laila had never heard Raisa call her *my daughter.* She was so shocked to hear those words that she missed part of the conversation.

"The museum called to say that an item was taken—was stolen—by one of our students," Mrs. Deere said.

"It wasn't me!" Laila exclaimed. Her face was flushed with a mixture of anger and humiliation. She rose up and stared from Mrs. Deere to her stepmom with indignation.

"Of course it wasn't Laila," Raisa interjected vehemently.

"I'm just as baffled, to be honest. But we cannot tell them that they're lying. I just want you to know that we are still investigating such a strong accusation," said Mrs. Deere. "We will keep you informed of the progress."

"I see, so nothing is definite then?" said Laila's step-mom, relaxing a little in her chair.

"We will let you know as soon as we hear more from the Museum," said Mrs. Deere. "I appreciate you taking the time. We have full confidence in the investigative process."

"I have full confidence in *my daughter*," Laila's stepmom said, as she stood up to leave. "Good day to you," she said, a little stiffly, as she shook hands with the principal and walked out of the office with Laila.

"Don't worry," she reassured Laila. "It will all soon be cleared up," she said, checking her watch. "The babysitter needs to leave by eleven. I need to get back soon. I'll see you later then, Laila." She hugged Laila. Laila felt a warmth awaken inside, as if she realized she wasn't alone. She still had family. With a wave and a smile, Raisa walked to her car. Laila turned and swung her backpack over her right shoulder and walked to class. Something had to be done today. Laila

was not going to wait for someone to decide if she was inno-
cent. She had to find a way to get to the museum and prove
her innocence.

CHAPTER 19
THE PLAN

"We have to believe in a greater plan," said Baba. "We have to believe there's more to the 'here and now,' and faith gives us that."

In the cafeteria at lunch, Laila shared her plan with Beth.

"We need to go to the Field Museum tonight," Laila said.

"How do we do that?" asked Beth, taking a bite of her sandwich. "We have another two years before we get our driver permits."

"I have a plan," said Laila. "We have to go this evening. I'll come over to your house for homework, then we'll ask your mom to drop us off at the library. We can walk to the station, get the train, and be there before it closes."

"You've got this all figured out," said Beth with admiration.

"It's kind of a life or death situation for me. I have no choice!" Laila muttered, "I need to prove my innocence. I need to find out what happened."

"Let's go for it then. Operation DNA—The Innocence Project!" Beth said, feeling clever.

"Look, our stories have to match: I'm coming over to

work on my report with you. Then both of us can 'go to the library' to study. Got it?" said Laila.

"Got it," said Beth, giving Laila a fist bump. "I'll see you after school, then."

"See you later," said Laila, grabbing her tray. "I've got Social Studies now."

Laila headed over to the Social Studies room. She wanted to see the teacher before class began.

"Ah, Laila," said Miss Levin, "I hope you have the report today, as promised."

"Yes, I've completed it. Thanks for the extra time, Miss Levin. I hope it won't affect my grade."

"No, you should be fine," Miss Levin said with a smile, something so rare that Laila stood and stared for a moment. "I wish more students were as concerned about their grades as you are." Laila took out her folder and handed it to Miss Levin. Her teacher took it to her desk and sat down to read, while the other students began shuffling into the class.

"Good afternoon Class," called Miss Levin. Laila looked at the clock and began counting down the minutes till the end of the school day.

The bell rang, and Laila grabbed her back pack, ready to leave.

"Laila, your report is fascinating," Miss Levin said. "If you have time after school today, I would like to talk about it. Perhaps you could do a presentation for the class. This is an interesting choice of an emancipator of women, and I think it would be a great learning experience for the class. What do you say? How about next week's morning assembly?"

"Thanks, Miss Levin, I've got plans this evening," Laila said. "Maybe tomorrow?"

"Sure," Miss Levin said. "It can wait another day."

Laila hurried out of the classroom, breathing a sigh of relief. Her last period was Math, then she would head out with Beth to her home, and then their secret operation would begin.

CHAPTER 20
TO THE MUSEUM

Laila stood cautiously at the doorway, wearing a purple dress. She held tightly onto Baba's hand on her first day of Kindergarten. She observed other children as they waved goodbye to their parent upon entering the classroom and moved to find their desks, where each child's name was written in bold and colorful letters. Laila waited. A girl walked in with her mother. She had brown hair, wore a purple dress, with a matching purple backpack on her shoulders. Laila's face lit up. She left Baba's side and ran over to the girl.

"Hi, I'm Laila," she said with a smile. "Purple's my favorite color."

"Mine too," the girl replied, with a shy smile. "I'm Beth."

"The day dragged on a bit, didn't it?" said Beth, when she met Laila at her locker after school.

"Yeah, I was watching the clock. It was like time slowed down," agreed Laila. She grabbed her books from the locker, slammed it shut, and headed out with Beth as planned.

They walked to Beth's house together. After a quick snack, Beth's mom dropped them off at the library. As soon as she drove away, they walked toward the train station.

Luckily, they caught a train headed for Chicago pretty quickly. Everything was going according to plan.

They reached Union Station and headed to the street where they hailed a cab. Beth had brought her savings to pay for the cab. They arrived at the Field Museum just before closing time but were allowed in, as they had passes. Laila brought her membership card. She held her breath as the attendant looked at both passes. She sighed with relief when no questions were asked, and they were handed stickers and went on their way. She knew her way around the museum. Beth followed as Laila led the way upstairs to the DNA lab. Laila was hoping she would meet Dr. Waldron. There was no one there. Laila and Beth stood, looking through the glass. The desks were all empty, as if everyone had gone home for the day.

"First, I need to use the restroom," Beth said, looking for signs to the restroom. Laila waited for Beth, while walking around the museum exhibits. She saw a sign that read: "Experience the Muslim Pilgrimage for the first time in 3D." She wandered across the hallway, into a dark room lit with ancient exhibits from the Middle East. Laila stood beside a miniature of a caravan in the desert, looking at the characters, some on camels while others walked beside them. She turned to a glass case with ornaments made of copper and clay. Beth must be wondering where she was, she thought, and turned to go back to the main hallway. Her hands became clammy, and she could barely see through the darkness. A breeze blew at her, and she knew something was not quite right. She heard sounds of laughter and turned her head to see Zaynab, looking much older. Her hair was gray at the temples, and her eyes creased into many lines when she smiled. Beside her stood Khalil, with a thick beard, though his eyes shone like stars, just as Laila remembered. His smile was warm and wide, just like his boyish grin. She was not dreaming, for she felt the humidity in the air, as if she were in a desert.

"You left without saying goodbye," Zaynab said and her smile brimmed with happiness.

"More importantly, you left before we could thank you," added Khalil.

"For what?" whispered Laila, faltering on her feet, reaching out to hold onto a wall that was no longer there. She touched the bark of a date palm tree, where the museum wall was just moments before. Her feet were sandaled, and she was dressed as Zaynab, in a long robe and shawl, standing in front of a stone building.

Khalil's head was bare, his thick salt and pepper hair curled long, resting on his shoulders.

"For transforming our lives—for all this," Khalil said, looking at Zaynab, who blushed shyly.

"Twenty years have passed, but we never forgot you," said Zaynab. "Omie passed away two years ago, but Laila is grown now, thanks to you and God's mercy."

"Had you not brought us to Medina," Khalil said, "we would never have found the Messenger of God. We would never have found this life we have now enjoyed these twenty years."

Just as they came, as a vision, so they vanished. Laila was left staring at an exhibit of copper utensils dating back to the Middle Ages. She pressed her hands to her face, which was wet with tears. "She lived," Laila whispered. "Baby Laila lived."

Her phone buzzed with a text from Beth. "Where R U?"

Laila met Beth by the stairs outside the restrooms. She could not think about this yet, she had to sort out her present predicament first.

"We'll have to search the whole museum now," said Laila. It was a chance she was willing to take, even though she was not sure whether she would find her in time, before the museum closed. She smiled every time she thought of the baby who lived. An announcement rang out on the PA system: The museum will be closing in fifteen minutes.

"We need to hurry," Beth said, getting nervous.

"We just need to find Dr. Waldron from the science department," Laila said, trying to sound casual, but she was beginning to realize things were more complicated.

"What'll we do if we don't find her in time?" asked Beth, in a low voice. "She may have left for the day."

"Let's try to be positive," Laila said. "So far, all is going to plan. Well, nearly."

The clock told her that their plans would need to change if they didn't find her as soon as possible.

"We may need to wait until late," said Laila, though she had not counted on being there when the museum closed for the night. Slowly, the crowds of visitors dwindled as the hustle and bustle of people died down.

"You mean we're going to, like, spend the night at the museum?" Beth asked. "This is not going to look good."

"We won't be able to get back home in time," Laila said, her voice shook. She was getting nervous now. She hadn't quite thought her plan all the way through to the end.

"Can I help you ladies?" Beth and Laila were taken aback. Standing in front of them was none other than the scientist they were hoping to meet. "The Museum is closed now. Shouldn't you be heading downstairs?" asked Dr. Waldron.

"Actually... we were looking for you," said Laila as relief flooded through her after the initial shock of seeing the scientist. "We wanted to ask you a few questions, if you can spare us five minutes of your time?"

"Well, I am working right now, if you can be quick

about it... Were you not here a few days ago on a school field trip?" asked Dr. Waldron.

"Yes, that's why we're here. You see, I've been accused of stealing. We're here to find out why," said Laila. "I didn't steal anything..." she stammered.

"Follow me," said Dr. Waldron. "I remember now. There was a sample sent for DNA testing, that was strange. As you know, your class was fortunate to be part of a new study that can do what carbon dating does, but much more thoroughly and, more importantly, much more cheaply. It will mean huge strides for science. I did this as a favor to my big sister, your Science teacher. She was the one that got me interested in science."

"Yes, she's a great teacher. She gets students excited with her enthusiasm," said Laila nodding.

"Yep, that's our Mrs. Mullings. Her excitement rubs off on us," said Beth.

"So, Laila," said Dr. Waldron, "the sample you gave was dated to being fourteen hundred years old, and it was from a specific region in the Middle East. That's how precise our new technology is."

"Wow!" said Beth, her mouth wide open.

Laila stood speechless for a moment.

"So one of the junior interns tried to be smart and said it was stolen from the Antiquities section. The school was notified of this. It's a serious situation," said Dr. Waldron, "I've been working on figuring this out today, so it's quite opportune that you girls showed up. I have something to share with you."

Beth and Laila followed Dr. Waldron to her office. She opened a folder on her desk. Laila's name was clearly written on the folder. Beth and Laila looked at the folder, then exchanged glances.

"First, I want you to be absolutely honest with me,"

said Dr. Waldron. "What I am about to share with you is pretty amazing, and you can't dispute science. We have confirmed the results many times to be sure."

"Yes, we'll answer any questions you have," Beth said quickly.

"I just want to clear my name. I didn't steal anything," Laila added.

"The sample you gave, Laila, did not have any roots on the hair, so until recently, we would not have been able to use it as a sample. Now however, with the amazing break-through in science that I keep mentioning because it's so awesome," said Dr. Waldron looking a lot more like her sister, "the findings show us that this hair belongs to a newborn female from the seventh century Arabia. That is how amazingly accurate we can get."

Beth's mouth dropped open as Laila drew in her breath. "They called the school right away, assuming the sample was stolen from our museum Antiquities collection. He should have waited to clarify, but he was angry and jumped to the wrong conclusion. I'm sorry you had to go through this. I wanted to pursue this, so I researched and saw that this sample was not from our collection," Dr. Waldron paused, and looked at Laila.

"Laila, I know you didn't steal this, as we do not have any samples from this particular period in time," she said.

"So, did you call the school?" asked Laila, relief flooding through her.

"I will call first thing tomorrow morning," answered Dr. Waldron, with a smile. "Now, I want to know how you came about finding this sample of hair?"

"It was a gift," said Laila, "from the mother of the baby." Laila looked at Beth, who nodded, and she began her story. Dr. Waldron listened quietly.

When Laila had related the events leading up to where

Omie had given her the baby's lock of hair, she said, "There are more things in heaven and earth than are dreamt of..."

"You believe us—our story?" Beth asked.

"Let's just say, I'm open to possibilities. There is so much in science that continues to amaze me. Scientific inquiry is like a tool that helps to unlock the mysteries of the universe," said Dr. Waldron.

Laila remembered Baba's words as Dr. Waldron continued, "The more I learn, the more I become increasingly aware of how little we know. There's so much more to learn, and there are many theories on time travel. I would not rule anything out. I became a scientist because of Dr. Who and Star Trek. My sister always told me stories as a child. It's why I am who I am."

Laila and Beth were suddenly aware of the time, and how late it was getting.

"Mom's probably waiting for us at the library," Beth said.

"We need to be getting back," said Laila.

"I'm pretty much done here for the day if you ladies need a ride? I'm happy to take you home and help explain things to your mothers if needs be," Dr. Waldron said. The relief on their faces was answer enough.

CHAPTER 21
SAFE AT LAST

TEN-YEAR-OLD LAILA WALKED *into the house after being dropped off, having attended Beth's birthday party.*

"Salaam, Beti. How was the party?" asked Baba, putting down his book.

"Fine," said Laila, pouting moodily.

"Did you enjoy yourself?" asked Baba. Laila shrugged her shoulders impatiently.

"Baba, why don't you know more about girls' stuff?" Laila asked.

"I'm sorry Beti, I guess you're right. I have no idea about girls' stuff," said Baba, deep in thought. "Perhaps I should do something about it, my Jaan."

THERE WAS A KNOCK AT THE DOOR. LAILA'S STEPMOM walked into the room holding a box. Naila crawled into the room, gurgling with her wide, gummy smile. Laila smiled back at her. She hadn't noticed how cute Naila had become. She crawled over to Laila as her smile widened, spreading across her face. Laila felt her heart tug. *She's my sister, my half-*

sister, but still my sister. She will never know Baba. Laila felt a pang of guilt. She had blamed a baby for her missed opportunity of going on pilgrimage with Baba. They had to cancel due to her stepmom's pregnancy. Laila's resentment had built up with each day, until it consumed her. What does Naila have to do with anything? Laila smiled at Naila.

"While I was packing, I found this," Laila's stepmom said. "These are your Baba's books. He would want you to have them." She placed the box on Laila's desk, then scooped Naila into her arms and quietly stepped out of the room. Balancing Naila on her hip, she closed the door behind her.

Laila put down her jeans on the pile of laundry she had been folding and walked over to the desk. The box was a cardboard filing box from an office supply store. She lifted the lid. There were books, papers, and some pens. She touched the spines on the old books from Baba's collection. She pulled out a book of Tennyson's poems. It was worn and old, an antique copy. She felt the pages reverently, then closed the book and picked up another. David Copperfield by Charles Dickens. She smiled, remembering when Baba read the entire book to her when she was in fifth grade. Each of the books brought back some special memory. Laila placed the books back into the box.

A sealed envelope caught her eye. She lifted it out and sat cross-legged on her floor. It was addressed to her. Baba's handwriting was scrawled in his familiar cursive, bold angular strokes in black ink. She sniffed the envelope, trying to breath in something more of his memory. She gently broke the seal and pulled out a letter. Her heart skipped a beat, as she read what was written:

"MY DARLING BETI LAILA,
If you are reading this, it's most likely I'm no longer in this world.

Please be strong—we cannot always understand God's Plan, but we must believe there is a greater plan for us. Don't grieve too much, for I'm with your mother now. Your sadness will be great, but you must find faith and courage to live your life to the fullest. I have only left you in body. My darling Beti and my love—our love —will always be with you, no matter where you are. Remember that. God is most merciful. Live with an open heart, live with a bond with your Creator, so that when you return to Him, it will be like coming home. I'm sorry life is hard for you right now. The reason I married again was not to replace your mother, but to give you some companionship that a mother would provide. Raisa's a lot like I imagine you will be when you grow up. Please give her a chance. She's known much pain and loss. I hoped to give her a second chance at happiness and hope you will become friends. Take care of your sister. I know I do not need to ask this, for I know you will love her more than I can imagine. You have a good, kind heart. Be her companion, her friend, her guide. Until we meet again, my dearest. I leave you all my love and all my prayers...

Baba

CHAPTER 22
FORECLOSURE

LAILA FOUND her stepmother in the kitchen, packing boxes. They were to leave in two weeks. They had found a two-bedroom apartment, and Raisa wanted to be out before the house was foreclosed.

"I'm glad the misunderstanding was cleared up," Laila's stepmom said.

"Thank you for sticking up for me," Laila said. "Thank you for the box. I know you miss Baba too. I'm sorry for being selfish and thinking only of myself."

"I understand. I was your age when I lost my father," said her stepmom.

Laila looked at her stepmom, feeling she never really saw her as a person, but as someone who was trying to replace her mother.

"We can be a family—just the three of us. I'm not trying to replace your mom. I'm just trying to do the best I can. We can do this together."

Laila nodded, "It's what Baba wanted for me—for us. I'm sorry... *Ammi*."

Laila's stepmom smiled. She had waited two years to

hear the word mother, *Ammi*. She walked up to Laila and gave her a big hug. Laila saw the pendant around her neck. She gasped as goosebumps crawled along the back of her neck. It was exactly the same as the pendant that Omie had worn, Laila remembered.

"Are you okay?" Raisa asked, her voice was gently concerned. Laila shook her head, staring at the pendant, as if mesmerized. "Do you like my pendant?" Raisa smiled.

"Where did you get it?" Laila whispered, "It's very unusual."

"It was passed down through my family for generations. You know, if you weren't named Laila, I would have given that name to Naila?" Raisa said.

"Oh, why?" Laila asked, curious to know. Raisa shook her head with a smile.

"It sounds silly, but for generations the first daughter born in my family has been named Laila. Call it what you will," she said as she took off the pendant hanging from her neck. It hung on a gold chain. "This locket has been passed down for centuries." Laila gasped. Surely this was too big of a coincidence, but it looked very much like the medallion that hung around Omie's neck.

"I know it sounds crazy, doesn't it," Raisa continued. "They say one of our ancestors was named Laila. Tradition has it that a stranger saved her life from the barbaric customs of the time, when baby girls were buried alive. Somehow her family escaped and were taken safely to Medina."

Goosebumps curled up Laila's arms. It couldn't be possible. She listened quietly.

"My family moved to Pakistan couple of centuries ago. We originally came from Medina, the city of the Prophet," Raisa said looking at Laila. "I don't know why, but I just thought I'd share that story with you. It sounds like a pretty fantastical tale don't you think?"

"It's a beautiful story," said Laila. "There might be some truth to it." She remembered Baba's words, "Everything happens for a reason."

Aloud she said, "There are more things in heaven and earth than are dreamt of..."

Raisa looked at Laila, her face confused.

"Shakespeare," said Laila.

"Oh, yes," said Raisa, "Hamlet."

CHAPTER 23
THE EMERGENCY-ROOM

LAILA STOOD IN A GARDEN. A beautiful breeze blew, rustling through branches of trees and shrubs, as if whispering secrets. Flowers of all hues were in abundance, some she had never seen before: bright, bold, dazzling in their flamboyance. It was as if Laila had stepped into a meadow in a land of dreams. It was too beautiful to be true, she thought as she walked on a path through the greenest lawn bordered with golden lilies. The air was heavy with the scent of the rose. Its sweetness lulled her mind into a state of euphoria. She was meeting someone. That was all she knew. She was invited to a feast. Beyond the garden path was a great opening, encircled by trees. A long table spread lay before her—a magnificent feast. Many people sat at the table. At the head of the table sat her father. Beside him sat her mother, just as she looked in the one photograph Laila had of her. Baba looked at her and smiled. His hair was black—gone were the grey hairs and lines of worry that once etched his forehead. He called to Laila. There was an empty seat beside him and her mother. "Laila." He called her name again and motioned to the empty chair beside him. Laila's heart fluttered, she breathed in the sweet fragrance in the air where the feeling was one of exultant joy and deep serenity. Laila quickened her steps.

"Baba...?" she whispered.

The people around the table seemed familiar, yet unfamiliar, her grandparents and great grandparents and relatives she had never known. All she knew was that Baba was there, just a few steps away from her. She quickened her steps toward the table. When she was barely two feet away from Baba, an invisible barrier arose between her and the table of guests. Laila tried to move forward, but her feet would not allow her. She was frozen in one spot. She looked at Baba. He saw her sadness and reassured her with a smile. He shook his head, as if to say, "Not yet, Laila Beti. It's your time to live on this earth."

"Baba!" she cried.

Laila awoke. Her pillow was damp with tears. She sat up in bed, trying to make sense of her dream; she was disturbed by it, yet comforted.

"Baba's okay. He will wait for me," she whispered. The clock showed it was five past midnight. Laila looked at the full moon from her window. She heard Naila's continuous crying. She had never paid attention before. She knew her stepmom would take care of Naila. This time was different. The cry was different. Laila slipped out of bed ran to the nursery. Her stepmom was rocking Naila, who wouldn't stop crying.

"Is she okay?" Laila asked, seeing her stepmom's eyes were red from lack of sleep.

"She's burning up with a fever," her stepmom whispered. "I've given her medicine, but it doesn't help." Naila cried, her face was red and blotchy.

"Would you like me to take her?" Laila asked. Her stepmom gently handed Naila into her arms. Laila realized she had never held her sister since the day she was born, when Baba handed the seven-pound new-born into her arms. She was a lot bigger now at ten-months. Laila cradled her in her arms. Naila was inconsolable. She pushed at Laila restlessly as her face burned with fever.

"I'm taking her to the ER," said her stepmom. "This isn't just a fever from a common cold—its been going on for too long."

"I'm coming with you," Laila said, grabbing the car keys as her stepmom wrapped Naila in a thin cotton shawl.

The drive to the hospital seemed like an eternity, they could not get there fast enough.

"We should have called an ambulance," her stepmom said as her voice shook with fear.

Laila's heart sank as Naila continued to cry. Her stepmom drove as Laila tried consoling Naila with soothing words of comfort. She tried giving her a pacifier; it didn't work. She offered her water in a sippy-cup. Nothing worked.

They arrived at the ER. Parking the car, Raisa grabbed the baby, Laila took her bag, and they rushed through the sliding doors. Nurses greeted them immediately and asked questions about Naila's condition.

"We're not busy tonight, so she should be seen right away," said the nurse on duty, recognizing the urgency, and took them straight into a cubicle. Everything happened fast. Naila was hooked up to an IV and monitor. Nurses and doctors entered in and out as the night progressed. Naila was taken to the PICU immediately after being seen by the doctor. Her temperature continued to spike. It seemed a nightmare as Laila helplessly watched the terror-stricken face of her baby sister and the worn and anxious face of her stepmom. Her condition did not improve even after several medications were administered through her IV. Laila and Raisa sat by Naila's bedside all night. Exhausted, Naila had finally fallen asleep. Her fever subsided momentarily, but then rose again. Her face was flushed, and her body burned to the touch. Laila and Raisa sat, helplessly watching little Naila's jagged breathing as her tiny body lay there with wires taped to her arms and chest, plugged to monitors and machines. The night staff came to ask if they would take some rest. Laila could not even think of sleeping.

Laila felt the tectonic plates of her world were shifting again and she felt she would fall into the crevices somewhere deep, where there was darkness devoid of hope. She had been there before when Baba died. She was falling. She needed something to help pull her out. She needed something to hold onto. Faith. Baba's faith had sustained him when her mother died. Laila remembered his words: "We don't control life and death, it is in God's hands. We have to submit to our Creator, then have hope things will work out for the best."

Laila could lose the only sister she had. She would never forgive herself for blaming her baby sister, for something she wasn't even aware of. She was a baby who would never know Baba, their father. It was up to Laila to share her memories with her sister. At least, she promised herself she would if Naila recovered and came home. *Please let her be well. Please let me have my sister back.*

CHAPTER 24
A NEW BEGINNING

Laila went to the hospital restroom. At the sink she performed the ritual ablution for prayer, *wudu,* washing her hands three times, then her face and arms up to the elbow. She walked downstairs to the chapel, where she faced the *kiblah*, the direction of the Kaaba in Mecca, and prayed like she had never prayed before. She forgot she was in a chapel. She forgot she was in a hospital. She forgot everything, except that she stood before her Creator and begged Him for her sister to be well again. As she bowed her head to the ground in *Sujood,* she prayed with all her heart. The ball of grief and resentment melted away and opened her heart to the grace of God. She felt rather than heard the reassuring words, *I am listening. All you need to do is ask and I hear you. I am waiting to answer your prayers.*

Laila prayed. She felt something alter in her, as peace entered her heart. The muscles in her whole body relaxed, and she felt calmer. After praying, Laila left the chapel in search of Raisa. She found her in the PICU, fast asleep with her head resting on the bed beside Naila's hand.

"Her fever has come down, dear," said the nurse. "The

doctor says we have to wait a few days and see how she responds to the antibiotics, but she's in good hands." The nurse smiled, "It's pneumonia, and they caught it at the right time. Bless her heart. You get some rest now. There's another chair by the bed if you like."

"Thank you," Laila said with a shaky smile. She sank into the chair, leaning back and drifted off to sleep.

Laila awoke after an hour or so. Raisa was standing by the bed, watching Naila as she slept peacefully.

"You need to get some rest, the both of you. We are here with the baby," said the staff nurse. "You go for some coffee and a bite to eat." Raisa and Laila both reluctantly left the PICU and walked down the corridors of the hospital, quiet and eerie in the middle of the night. They passed very few paramedics as they walked through the hallway and into an elevator. The cafeteria was closed, so they grabbed coffee from the dispenser in the hallway at the hospital entrance. There were chairs near the window. They sank into the cushioned seats and sipped coffee in silence.

They talked as the white light of dawn lit up the velvet darkness of the departing night. Moonlight shone through the windows, and the bustle and sounds of a new day began as a hymn on the street below. Laila had never spoken much to Raisa in the two years she had known her. She hadn't really got to know her. She had closed herself up. When Baba died, she bottled up all her resentment and grief. She had allowed it to become a heavy load in her heart.

When Raisa and Laila returned to the PICU, Naila was still sleeping. Laila looked at her long lashes as she slept. She thought of her dream. She had thirteen years with Baba. Naila would never know him. It was up to Laila to teach her all that Baba had taught her. She would be a responsible big sister. She would show her how to hula hoop and help her with homework. She smiled. First things first. Naila needs to learn to walk first. And talk. And read. She would read all the books that Baba read with her. Laila smiled at the thought.

Hope sprang into her heart. Nothing was certain after all, but she was alive. This was her life. It was up to her how she lived it. She felt a warmth inside her, something she couldn't explain. She felt if she put words to it, that would somehow limit what it was and make it less significant. She looked at the new day, blazing with glory outside, and smiled. *Faith is something you can't see; you feel it inside of you— and that's what matters. I don't need proof. I know it. It's in my heart. There's a plan, and it will all work out in the end. Insha'Allah. God-willing.*

Life was unpredictable, but this was her life. This was her time.

A YOUNG MOTHER HELD A SMALL BUNDLE WRAPPED IN A PINK blanket. She smiled as she looked at her newborn baby girl.

"She's the most beautiful baby in the world," said the father, a young man seated beside his wife's bedside. He leaned over and gently touched the baby's cheek. "I never thought I could feel this way about such a tiny creature."

"You're going soft, Habeebi," said the mother and she smiled with a twinkle in her eye. "She has your nose."

"And your eyes," said the father.

"I feel my heart is so full, I can't imagine being happier," said the mother.

"You are going to go to the best college," said the father, talking to the baby who had been in this world barely five hours. "Yes, you are my precious. You will be the smartest, kindest, most compassionate soul," his voice shook with emotion. "May Almighty God protect and guide you always."

A nurse entered the hospital room. She smiled at the picture of the young family. She had seen this emotional setting many times in her years at the hospital—another young couple with their first child.

"She has a nice head of hair on her," said the nurse. "Have you chosen a name yet?"

"Laila," said the mother, looking up at the nurse. "Her eyes are dark as night, with the sparkle of stars in them."

"A beautiful name for a beautiful baby. Congratulations," said the nurse as she reached over to take the baby. "I'm just going to check her temperature. Don't worry, she will be back in your arms soon enough. You will then have all the time in the world to hold her."

……………………………………………………………………

AFTERWORD

According to Islamic tradition, Adam and Eve were the first humans sent to live on earth. After wandering the earth, they were reunited in Mecca where Adam—the first Prophet of Islam—built the original Kaaba for worshipping the one Almighty God. Many Messengers or Prophets were sent to guide people in moments of dire need, when societies experienced extreme ignorance and injustice, such as in Seventh Century Arabia. Muhammad (May the peace and blessings of God be with him) was the last Messenger, known as the Seal of all the Prophets—from Adam, Noah, Abraham, Moses, to Jesus. Muslims believe he was given the final revelation of God, which contained the same message as the previous Messengers plus more specific details on how to live a righteous and good life. There are over one billion Muslims throughout the world who follow the religion of Islam. Islam means "peace, through submission to God." In other words, when one believes in the One Creator of all living things and all the universe, then one submits to His authority and finds peace. Muslims pray five times a day, facing Mecca. The five prayers— Fajr, Zhuhr, Asr, Maghrib, and Isha—are one of the five pillars of the Islamic faith. Fasting, the giving of charity, and going on the annual pilgrimage of Hajj are three more pillars. The first pillar is belief in one God.

Abraham rebuilt the Kaaba centuries after it had been destroyed, when it was a barren desert. The Station of Abraham in Mecca is said to contain his footprint.

Muslims all over the world seek to visit Mecca on pilgrimage. One of the rituals of pilgrimage includes following in the footsteps of Abraham's wife, Hagar, as she ran from hill to hill, searching for water in the parched desert. The well of Zamzam is said to have sprung out when the Angel Gabriel came to help the thirsty and crying baby Ishmael. Today, pilgrims drink from the well of Zamzam. It is known as a miracle well that has never run dry in thousands of years.

GLOSSARY

- **Abaya:** Long robe worn by women
- **Ammi:** Mother (Urdu)
- **Abi:** My father (Arabic)
- **Adhan:** Call to prayer in Arabic
- **Assalaamu' Alaikum:** Arabic greeting, meaning Peace be with you
- **Baab:** Doorway
- **Baba:** Father
- **Bhabi:** Brother's wife (Urdu)
- **Fi-Amaan Allah:** God protect you
- **Habibi:** Dearest (Endearment in Arabic)
- **Hajj:** Annual Pilgrimage to Mecca
- **Hijab:** Headscarf or head-covering worn by women
- **Hejaz:** What is now known as the Kingdom of Saudi Arabia
- **Hajar-al-Aswad:** The Black Stone that is set in one corner of the Kaaba. Tradition has it that it was handed to Abraham by Angel Gabriel, when he rebuilt the Kaaba.

- **Jaan:** Life (endearment in Urdu)
- **Jahiliah:** Age of ignorance
- **Kaaba:** The first house of worship of one God to be built on earth. Tradition has it that Adam built the Kaaba after he and Eve were reunited after leaving paradise. It was later rebuilt by Abraham and his son.
- **Kiblah:** The direction of the Kaaba. Muslims around the world face the Kiblah from all corners of the earth, when they pray five times a day.
- **La-ilaha-illallah:** There is no deity but the God (Arabic article of faith)
- **Layth:** Boy's name (Arabic) meaning Lion
- **Maasha'Allah:** As God has made it (said when praising something)
- **Medina:** Yathrib came to be renamed Medina, the city of the Messenger of God.
- **Meccans:** People of Mecca
- **Miqat:** "A stated place"- where pilgrims prepare for Umrah or Hajj
- **Muslim:** Literal meaning: one who submits
- **Omie:** My Mother (Arabic)
- **Qasidah:** ballad (Arabic)
- **Shukran:** Thank you (Arabic)
- **Sujood:** Prostration—a part of prayer with the forehead touching the ground
- **Tawaf:** Circumambulating the Kaaba
- **Umra':** The shorter pilgrimage
- **Wadi:** Reservoir, where rain water collects in the desert
- **Wa-Rahmatullah:** And Blessings of God (Arabic greeting)
- **Yathrib:** The city that later came to be called Medina

- **Zamzam:** The water-well, which for centuries has provided water for pilgrims in Mecca.

ACKNOWLEDGMENTS

It is often said that it takes a village to raise a child. The same adage can be applied to the process of bringing a book into the world. I could not have done this without the support of so many. I do not know how I can even begin to express the feeling except with a humble heart overflowing with gratitude for all who helped and supported me on this journey. I want to thank my publisher, Callie Metler, for believing in Laila. I felt like a parent feels when their child is praised. I want to thank Austin Ruh for his insight in editing the story from its early stages to where it now stands.

I wish to thank my mother, to whom I owe everything, and honor the memory of my father, gone from this world but never forgotten.

I want to thank my children, Nadia, Sabeen and Shaheed, for reading my manuscript and for their love and support throughout the whole process. I wrote it for you. My husband Talha, who is my best friend and greatest supporter, who believed in me and my work as a writer even before I did, and has encouraged me wholeheartedly with endless and unconditional love.

Thank you to my niece, Ayesha for reading the final draft, to my sisters, Yasmin, Afshan, Shahin and Asma. To my brothers, Ibrahim and Omar for invaluable advice and suggestions, and I am especially grateful to Omar for creating the beautiful cover. Thank you also to my nieces, nephews, great-nieces, great-nephews, family and friends across the world for their love and support for my dream of bringing Laila into the world.

A heartfelt thank you to Nadia Malik, who was one of the first to read the completed manuscript. Thank you my dear friend Dawne Salier, for reading through the entire manuscript. Many years ago, when the idea of Laila first came to me, my friend Zehra gave me some books to help with research. I honor her memory with unending gratitude, for she began this story's journey with me.

My critique groups have been overwhelmingly supportive in my journey, with wisdom and insight and invaluable advice. You have become dear and treasured friends since our writing journey brought us together - thank you all.

The kid lit community is the most generous and giving, I feel this is my community and it is the best place to be. Thank you to all my network of writer friends and colleagues. It is such an honor to be writing for the most important people in the world.

During my research, I spoke to many professionals for advice by phone and in person. I was welcomed at the Field Museum DNA center and even though I asked the silliest of questions, I received the most wonderful welcome and support. I am forever in your debt.

If I were to thank each of you individually it would take the space of another few chapters, so suffice it to say, please know how much I appreciate and value your support and help along this journey. Thank you. Thank you, one and all.

ABOUT THE AUTHOR

Shirin was born and raised in the UK, and now makes her home in the Chicago suburbs. Laila and the Sands of Time is her debut middle-grade novel. Shirin has raised six children- three human and three cats- all of whom have provided much inspiration for her stories. When she is not writing, Shirin enjoys reading, oil painting, and spending time with family.

Through the ever-changing
and ever-changeable Time
That was once Mine.